Posh... J. BAMFORD

DEATH
M...

Mark Hebden

10r

KEYHOLE CRIME
London · Sydney

First published in Great Britain 1979
by Hamish Hamilton Limited

Copyright © 1979 by Mark Hebden

Australian copyright 1982

This edition published 1982 by
Keyhole Crime, 15–16 Brook's Mews,
London W1A 1DR

ISBN 0 263 73958 9

Set in 10 on 10½ pt Linotron Times
06/0782

Photoset by Rowland Phototypesetting Ltd
Bury St Edmunds, Suffolk
Made and printed in Great Britain by
Cox & Wyman Ltd, Reading

CHAPTER
ONE

It wasn't a day for thinking of death.

After a series of heavy downpours that had left the place chill with damp, it had suddenly become warm—a day for thinking of young girls in their summer dresses, of children playing with dogs, of old men dropping steel spheres in the dust under the trees in a long slow game of boules; of summer air full of acrid cigarette smoke and the smell of vegetation burning in busy back gardens.

Inspector Pel ought to have known better. He'd been at the game long enough never to take things at their face value, and he ought to have realised that fate has a habit of doing sneaky things; that, with the windows open and even a faint breeze to take away the heat, it was a perfect morning for him to find himself dragged out of his comfortable office to stand on his feet until they felt as if they belonged to six other men—all cripples.

The sun in that part of France has a special quality of gold in it, and that morning it was streaming through Pel's window like the glory of the Lord. Across the city, the pale stone of the Palace of the Dukes, no longer a prestigious home but a mere headquarters for the local authorities, was glowing in the sunshine and the sound of the traffic was muted. Beyond the nearby wall, he could see a tiled roof, varnished and patterned in the manner for which the province was so rightly famous. Below, the parking area alongside the railway track was brilliant with the colours of parked cars.

The city had been the provincial capital since the Dark Ages and its rulers had challenged even the kings of France. If it seemed at times to belong to the Grand Siècle and the era of Louis XV and XVI, in out-of-the-way corners or behind the blank façades of its narrow streets there were still mediaeval relics that gave it a feeling of historical

continuity. It was a heart-warming city and a place to cheer
even a misanthrope like Pel.

Sitting at his desk, staring at a pile of dossiers, he was
trying his best to be bad-tempered. Thin-faced, dark-eyed
and intense, being bad-tempered was one of Pel's few
pleasures. He was unmarried, so there was nowhere he
could work out his frustrations except in the office. Even at
home he was bullied by his housekeeper.

He smoked too much, he knew, and had often tried to be
like Maigret and take to a pipe. But it left him with a sour
mouth and—because of the paraphernalia it necessitated
him carrying around—bulges in his clothes. Being neat
enough to dislike sagging suits, instead he worked his way
regularly through packets of Gauloises, trying to persuade
himself, despite the evidence to the contrary, that they
couldn't possibly do him any harm. He'd been told that,
although they were strong, they contained less saltpetre
than other cigarettes and that it was saltpetre that caused
cancer, though it still didn't alter the fact, as he well knew,
that they contained enough tar content to asphalt the N71
from Dijon to Châtillon.

He sighed, knowing he was weak, and lighting up his
third since he'd arrived, he dragged down the smoke so
deeply it looked as if it were about to emerge through his
ears, out of the ends of his sleeves and trouser bottoms,
even through his flies. The depth of the breath he drew in
nearly made his eyes fall out but, as he waved away the
smoke, he sat back, relaxed and alive again. He had been
handling four cases at once—two assaults, one rape and the
dubious death of an SNCF employee called Giulle at
Marsonnay, and they had so occupied his attention for the
last month he'd been keeping them all in the air at once like
a juggler with his oranges. He now felt worn out.

Pel liked to feel worn out—it made him feel he was
succeeding at his job—but at last he could see the end of the
cases. All but the death of the railwayman, Giulle, had
suddenly cleared up very happily and he was looking
forward to the whole weekend free of work, to enable him
to get over it, to sleep and relax. It was Pel's firm conviction

that he was a poor sleeper and needed to catch up when he could. In fact, he didn't need much sleep and woke every morning at 5.30 as if to an alarm.

He took another drag at the Gauloise, wondering if he ought to let himself go mad enough to enjoy his lunch, and what he ought to order for the sake of his health. Like every adult in France, he had learned all about his anatomy at school and now spent most of his waking hours considering how best to keep it in proper working order. Perhaps tomatoes in oil, he decided placidly. To lubricate things. With an omelette and a small carafe of wine and a coffee to follow, which, unhappily, would not be decaffeinated. Then a calm afternoon browsing through reports and an early departure for home, with perhaps a pernod and an energetic game of dominoes at the Café de L'Est on the way for exercise. Maybe even a wild bout of boules. Despite the awesome prospect of having to face the wrath of his house-keeper, Madame Routy, life, he thought, might just—with a little push—be worth living for a while.

The door opened and Sergeant Darcy's head appeared.

'Yes?' The word came out as a bark and Pel's placid air disappeared like a puff of smoke in a high wind.

Darcy didn't turn a hair. Chiefly because everyone else refused to work with Pel, Darcy had been his assistant for a long time now and he knew how to handle him. Sometimes, even, he considered his superior a pain in the neck. How much better, he often thought, if their positions had been reversed and he'd been the inspector and Pel the sergeant. On the other hand, of course, everybody knew that the police force—like the army—was run by its sergeants and with Pel as a sergeant it would have been God help the Fourth Republic.

'Trouble,' he said.

Pel pushed his spectacles up on his forehead. 'What sort of trouble?' he asked.

Darcy shrugged. 'The duty dogsbody took it. Between two chapters of a dirty book he was reading and a few thoughts on his girlfriend, I suspect. It looks like a big one.'

'Well, go on, spit it out.'

'I'm trying to be laconic,' Darcy said calmly. 'You always say that when you ask for a report you don't want poetry readings. It's murder.'

Pel stared, his dark intense eyes seeming to Darcy to go red with anger. 'I was looking forward to a quiet weekend,' he pointed out coldly.

'Sorry, Patron. So was I. But the Commissaire dropped it on us.'

'How did he know I was free?'

'Sixth sense, I expect. It's at Aigunay-le-Petit; 6 Chemin de Champ-Loups. Off the Rue Clement-Rémy.'

'Who?'

'Woman called Chenandier. Somebody demolished her with a heavy instrument.'

'Demolished?'

'That's what it sounds like.'

'Merde alors!' Pel flung the dossiers aside without looking where they went and they slid off the end of the desk and fell to the floor in a flutter of sheets of paper. Darcy stared at them but made no attempt to retrieve them. Pel glared at him.

'Well, pick them up!'

'Certainly, Patron.' Having forced the request, Darcy cheerfully scooped the papers into a jumbled pile and placed them back on the desk. 'I'll get Nosjean to sort them out as we leave.'

'Nosjean's an idiot. He'll probably flush them down the lavatory by mistake.'

Darcy smiled placatingly. 'He tries hard, Patron. He's still a bit inexperienced. And he's in love.'

Pel was not inclined to make allowances—not even for Nosjean's love life. 'Put a bomb under his backside,' he said. 'Wake him up. And if it's experience he wants, he can take over that death at Marsonnay—the railwayman, Giulle. I'm too busy. Especially now. Tell him to ask around.'

'Yes, Patron.'

Pel had put out his cigarette, jabbing it savagely in the ash-tray. Just when he was enjoying it, too, he thought bitterly, extracting the utmost from his martyrdom. 'Well, come on,' he snorted. 'Get going. What about the car?'

'Waiting, Patron.'

'Photographers? Fingerprints? Doctor? Laboratory?'

'All laid on, Patron.'

Unable to find anything to complain about, Pel pushed his chair back with a scrape and stalked out of the office, his spectacles still up on his forehead, flattening the thin dark hair he scraped close to his skull. Darcy followed him, dumping the pile of tangled reports on Nosjean's desk.

'You're to sort that lot out, *mon brave*,' he said pontifically to the pink-faced young man who gaped at them. 'And make sure you get 'em right or he'll have you back pounding a beat in no time.'

'Who?'

'Evariste Clovis Désiré Pel himself. No less.' Darcy rolled his eyes. 'Désiré,' he said. 'Desired one! Dieu!'

As he climbed out of the car at Aigunay-le-Petit, Evariste Clovis Désiré Pel was firmly convinced that God had it in for him.

To start off with, he carried a burden which would have made the Garden of Eden seem like a cold day in the mountains. Evariste Clovis Désiré Pel. He'd often wondered what his mother and father had been thinking when they'd chosen the names. Evariste, Clovis, or Désiré on their own might have been all right, but together they were enough to make a man feel ill. He sometimes even wondered if they were the reason he'd never married. After all, he'd often thought, any girl looking misty-eyed across the pillow, all pink and pleased with herself, to ask 'Isn't it about time I got to know your name?' and getting 'Evariste Clovis Désiré Pel' as an answer, would more than likely fall out of bed laughing. In fact, one had and Pel had never been keen to repeat the performance.

And this morning—now—he felt as if the depression he'd been so valiantly fighting off from the minute he'd got out of bed was crowding in on him again because he'd picked up the details en route and didn't like the sound of what he'd heard. Attacks with blunt instruments were messy and usually necessitated tiptoeing round the corpse like a cat on wet pavements, while everyone in the department, the whites of their eyes showing like a startled foal's at the horror, got themselves on edge over the amount of blood there was about. Attacks with heavy instruments were never neat and tidy and the blood went everywhere—on the walls, the furniture, the carpets, even on the ceiling. They were untidy affairs and, a tidy man at heart, Pel didn't like untidy murders.

Aigunay-le-Petit was just outside the city to the southeast in the sloping vine country through which a tributary of the Saône meandered in vast loops among the rushes and willows. It was a large village made up of old farms, sagging stone walls and lopsided barns with ancient beams; but interspersed here and there among them were modern houses built since the war. They reminded Pel uncomfortably of the house he lived in himself, and because of it, that he was underpaid, had a long time to go for his pension, was sufficiently unattractive to the opposite sex to have remained unmarried, had no children to look after him in his old age, and no prospects of ever having enough money to provide for that old age. As his bitterness welled up and he considered himself neglected, he felt much better.

The Chemin de Champ-Loups was a narrow cul-de-sac with an unmade surface, heavily overhung with large trees and bushes. It joined the end of the Rue Clement-Rémy and grew narrower and narrower until it became merely a footpath that continued past a footbridge which crossed a stream, then went on to emerge among the bushes lining the edge of the main road that finally went up to Langres.

The policeman at the gate of Number 6 stepped aside as they swept past. The house was an old building of grey stone with wisteria and ivy growing over a wrought-iron porch. Long shuttered windows reached to the ground and, beyond, Pel could see a gravel path and a garden sloping gently down to the stream that glittered among a thick brush of reeds and willows. The house was set back from the road up a short winding drive ankle-deep in crushed pebbles that had made a luxuriously expensive crunch as the car edged across them.

There were three vehicles parked at the back of the house. A grey Renault, an old Deux Chevaux and a rather shabby British Mini.

A police sergeant was inside the hall. He looked harassed and not a little green.

'Whose are all the cars?' Pel demanded.

'Madame's,' the sergeant said. 'The housekeeper's and the daughter's.'

'See that they're not touched. Where's the body?'

The sergeant gestured and Pel noticed that he hung well back as though he had no desire to be confronted once more by it.

'It's enough to make you throw up in there,' he announced.

'Anybody in the place when it happened?'

'Just the daughter and a housekeeper, sir. The house-keeper sleeps on the third floor in a sort of suite under the eaves. The daughter has a flat with a separate entrance on the end of the house.'

'Well, stop looking as if you've lost your trousers and let's have 'em somewhere I can talk to 'em. What about the husband?'

The sergeant made an effort to pull himself together. Clearly he liked messy murders no more than Pel. 'He's away on business,' he said. 'He's a wine exporter. In Paris, I gather.'

'When did it happen?'

'We don't know for certain yet, sir. But it looks as though it was during the night. She was in her nightclothes. It looks as though she heard something and came down to investigate and found an intruder. I think there are some things missing.'

'What sort of things?'

'Jewels probably.'

'Well, say so,' Pel snapped. '"Things missing" could mean anything from kitchen utensils to virginities. How do you know?'

The sergeant stiffened. 'I had a quick look round—'

'Carefully, I hope.'

'Of course, sir. But I thought there might be someone else upstairs, hurt or dying.'

'And was there?'

'No, sir. But I found a drawer open in the bedroom. It might just have been where she kept her nail files, but on the other hand she might have had jewellery there, too. It's the sort of drawer she might use. There's a lock with a key in it.'

Pel nodded. 'Check it,' he said.

'Right, sir.'

'Find out. Exactly.'

'Yes, sir, of course.'

As the sergeant disappeared, Pel turned to Darcy, 'You'd better check up on the husband,' he said. 'Get him down here. And don't rely on that sergeant too much. He doesn't know what time of day it is. He'll stand around with his mouth open like one of the carp in the Tuileries gardens. You'll have to do things yourself.'

CHAPTER
TWO

The body was in the salon, an elegant room with a grand piano and a Louis XIV escritoire. The shutters were still closed so that the light was faded and greenish-looking, and the curtains moved slightly in the breeze that was coming in from the garden through the open french window. The stereo was still turning at the dead end of a record of *Rigoletto*. Pel switched it off and the clicking stopped.

'How long has this been on?'

Darcy put his hand on the machine. 'All night by the feel of it,' he said dryly. 'Orchestrated murder.'

Pel stood in the centre of the room. It had once been a calm attractive place but at that moment it looked vaguely like a slaughterhouse. Which, in a way, it was.

There seemed to be blood everywhere, soaked in a huge dried pool into the thick pile carpet, into the cushions of the elegant settee, on the curtains, on the walls, on the side of the piano. To say nothing of fragments of bone and shreds of flesh. It looked as though a lunatic had been at work.

Pel didn't like blood any more than the sergeant outside but he knew what he had to do. While Darcy remained outside, he picked his way carefully round the furniture, avoiding the dark stains, to stare down at the body. It was that of a woman about forty, though at that moment it was hard to say whether she were attractive or ugly, pleasant or a bitch, because her face and head were mere bloody pulp from which one eye stared in a squint up at Pel from among the stiffened tangle of dark hair.

Darcy put his head round the door to the hall. 'There's blood here and by the front door, Chief,' he said. 'As well as on the step outside the french window. There's also a little on the grass and the gravel of the drive. Then no more. It looks as though whoever did it went out through the french window, round the house and down the drive to the lane. He probably had a car there.'

'Find out if anyone saw one around last night. And get the garages to keep their eyes open for bloodstained interiors. Whoever did this must have had it all over him.'

'Right, Chief. By the way, her handbag's in the hall.'

'Check what's in it. And let's have the office making a check on laundries for bloodstained clothes. Have them check all cleaners and the dustbin people. There's so much blood around, there must be some on the clothes of whoever it was who did it. Probably hair, tissue, and fragments of bone as well. Also check tradesmen. See if she had visitors—what sort of men she knew. And get another sergeant out here.'

Darcy vanished and a moment later his voice came quietly from the hall where he was telephoning headquarters. When he returned, Pel was still staring at the body. It was naked except for a flimsy gown which was twisted about it and was covered with dried blood that had given it the consistency of cardboard.

'Krauss's on his way,' Darcy said.

'He's not very bright,' Pel pointed out.

Darcy sighed. 'We've got to have somebody, Patron.'

Pel indicated the corpse. 'Name?' he asked.

Darcy flicked his notebook open. 'Camille-Jeanne Che-nandier. Wife of Hervé Chenandier, wine exporter, of this address.'

'Know anything about her?'

'I've picked up a bit. She was a bit of a singer.' Darcy nodded towards the stereo and the record of *Rigoletto*. 'Not so hot really, but she'd sung in the chorus once or twice at the Paris Opera House before she was married. Since then she'd given a few recitals and done a bit of amateur work. Nothing more. The sergeant knows her. Always fancied she was better than she actually was, I gather.'

'Family?'

'One daughter, Odile. She's awaiting our attentions now if that sergeant's worth his stripes.'

'No other family?'

'I gather not, Patron. But there's a brother. Also lives in the village. There's a gardener as well, who doesn't appear to have turned up this morning.'

'Find them.'

Pel sniffed. There was a dead smell in the air. It was a strange phenomenon he always noticed. It wasn't the blood. It was just death. As if there were a decaying figure waiting in the corner of the room.

While he stared, taking everything in, the other cars arrived—Minet, the doctor; Prélat, the fingerprint expert; the photographers; and Leguyader and his laboratory assistants, who were to go through the place with a fine tooth-comb. They arrived in the hall in a bunch, heading for the salon as if they were going to a football match.

They were a pretty motley bunch who ought to have got on well with each other, but, like all Frenchmen, they were arrogant and took themselves too seriously, and each belonged to a different political party, one of the fifty-odd million—one for every adult in France—that made up the political whole of the country. In the office they spent all their time arguing at the top of their voices so that they always appeared to be on the point of seizing each other by the throat, and they were all going full bore as they swept down the corridor.

Pel stood in the doorway and stopped them dead. 'Steady on,' he said. 'You're not a lot of farmers. Just tread carefully.'

One of the photographers put his head round the door and pulled a face. 'Oh, mon Dieu,' he said. 'What is it? Crime of passion?'

'At the moment it looks like a stormy night in a butcher's shop. Don't let's have anything touched.'

As they crept in, aware of Pel's eye directed at them like the barrel of a shot gun, Pel spoke to Darcy. 'Take a look round the place upstairs,' he said. 'First, though, what did the handbag show?'

Darcy disappeared to the hall and returned to dump an expensive patent-leather handbag on the table. 'All the usual,' he said. 'But there's one interesting thing. A note. An assignation by the look of it.'

He spread a small sheet of paper in front of Pel. It said in green ball-point letters, *See you 10 p.m.*

'Whose is the writing?'

'I haven't identified it yet. It's not the girl's or the housekeeper's.' He nodded towards the corpse. '*Or* hers.'

'Find out whose it is,' Pel said. 'Anything else?'

'All the usual things women carry. Two handkerchiefs. Two lipsticks. Powder compact. Specs. Diary. A couple of kilos of small coins. Why do women always have so many small coins at the bottom of their handbags?'

'Do they?'

'My girlfriends always do. I think they toss 'em in when they're in a hurry shopping, and then forget 'em. They only remember 'em when the handbag gets too heavy to cart around. There are also two ten-franc notes. Around 50 frs altogether.'

Pel studied the expensive hangings and furniture. 'Not much for a woman as wealthy as this one seems to be,' he commented. 'Let's go and see what the sergeant's turned up.'

There were two women waiting in a small room lined with books, both sitting in deep green-leather armchairs. The sergeant waited importantly by the door.

'Got everything set up for you, sir,' he said.

Pel glanced at the two women waiting inside. They both looked nervous but calm.

'Must have been quite an effort,' he said, and the sergeant flushed.

Standing by the desk, he stared about him. The room was as elegant as the salon where the body was. The books were all old, backed with leather and well marked with gilt, as though the owner collected them carefully. The two women were watching him intently, one of them a small neat woman with dark alert eyes, the other a girl in her early twenties with mouse-coloured hair and a sad agitated look that was mixed with wariness.

'Names, please?' Pel asked.

'Quermel,' the dark woman said. 'Estelle Quermel.'

'Madame? Mademoiselle?'

'Madame. I'm a widow. I'm the housekeeper.'

'What does that mean?'

Madame Quermel shrugged, her face expressionless. 'It means I did everything. Washed. Cleaned. Cooked. Made the beds. Even sometimes helped with the garden.'

'It must be marvellous,' the girl said heavily, 'to feel so saintly.'

Pel ignored the comment. 'And you?' he asked.

The girl gave an almost imperceptible shrug and tears started to her eyes. 'Chenandier,' she said. 'Odile Chenandier. Unmarried. And never likely to be.' She directed a frightened glance towards the salon. 'I'm her daughter.'

Pel gestured. 'I'll see you separately.' He looked at the girl. 'We'll have you first, Mademoiselle. Perhaps you'd come into the kitchen.'

The girl followed him into the kitchen and sat down at the table.

She wasn't an ill-looking girl. She had good features but

her skin was sallow and, like so many young people, she apparently didn't believe in make-up when a little would have worked wonders. There were times, Pel thought, when naturalism could be carried too far.

She watched him warily, twisting her hands. 'Why?' she asked suddenly. 'Why?'

'Why what, mademoiselle?'

'Why my mother? Why was she killed?'

Pel gestured. 'That's something we hope to find out,' he said gently.

The girl seemed to writhe inside her clothes. 'But why her? Why should this happen to us?'

Pel let her work it out of her system before he spoke. 'Where were you when it happened?' he said eventually.

She answered him slowly, hesitatingly. 'In my flat, I suppose. She was in her wrap, so I suppose it must have happened during the night.'

'Were you in all evening?'

'Yes. I stayed in writing letters. To friends, you know.'

'Male or female?'

'Both.'

'Were there many?'

'Yes.'

'Can I see them?'

She gave him a startled look. 'Why?'

'Just a check, that's all. If there were a lot as you say, that would be reasonable proof that you *were* in.'

Her eyes fell. 'I haven't got them,' she said. 'I posted them this morning before you arrived. There's a box in the lane.'

Pel rubbed his nose thoughtfully. 'Did you hear no sound at all last night?' he asked.

'You can't hear a thing from my flat.' The girl looked nervous and on edge. 'She was playing opera on the stereo, anyway, so I wouldn't.'

'Did she often play records on the stereo?'

The girl gave him a worried glance. 'Only opera. She was mad about opera. She sometimes went to Paris to hear it. She was always going on about singing there.' Her eyes filled with tears and, despite her aggressive manner, Pel suspected she was frightened and lost.

'It was all show really,' she said. 'All this opera.'

'In what way?'

'It was just to impress people. I think she'd long since forgotten all she ever knew. She was really a very ordinary person.'

Pel thought for a moment. 'Who found her?' he asked.

The girl stirred and gave him another scared look, her eyes filling with tears once more. 'I did. I came in this morning. My flat has a separate entrance in the drive and a door into this part of the house. I was going into the city and I was in need of cash. I never seem to have any. My father's a bit tight with it and keeps me short. As I reached the door I heard the stereo clicking and thought she was in here. Then I saw the blood and then her. So I stopped where I was and went to the kitchen to telephone the police.'

'Was this before or after you posted your letters?'

'Before.' She shook her head. 'No, after.' She gave a forlorn gesture. 'I don't remember.'

'Did you go into the room where she was?'

'No.'

'What time was this?'

'Around eight o'clock.'

'See anything unusual?'

The tears welled up again and the muddy skin grew pink. 'I'd have said my mother with her head smashed in was unusual, wouldn't you?' she said with an unexpected show of spirit.

Pel had meant footprints or disturbed furniture but he shrugged and didn't pursue the subject. He lit a cigarette slowly and drew the smoke down to his socks. His relations, when he bothered to visit them, which wasn't often, said he smoked so much he smelled like a Paris taxi. He waved away the blue wraiths round his head, fighting to get his breath as the acrid Régie Française tobacco clutched him by the throat, and watched the girl for a while. She was managing to hold back the persistent tears and so far there had been no expressions of sorrow, but Pel suspected she wasn't half as tough as she tried to make out and was terrified.

'Were you fond of your mother?' he asked.

She stared.

'Some daughters aren't.'

She blinked. 'Yes, I was.'

'Did you share things with her?'

She sighed. 'Not much,' she admitted. 'She was—well, she wasn't interested in the things I was interested in. I didn't like music, for instance. I didn't like her friends. But—well—' she gestured.

'But you got on all right?'

'Are you suggesting—?'

'I'm suggesting nothing, Mademoiselle. I just wish at this stage to know where people were and who they were with.'

She sighed again. 'I was alone. I told you. I don't like being alone.'

'Wasn't Madame Quermel in?'

'No. Nor the night before! I watched her leave from my window.'

'Do you often watch?'

'Yes.'

'Why?'

'I don't know.' The narrow shoulders moved hopelessly. 'Seeing people go out—you know—it's not much fun being alone.'

'Are you often alone?'

'Yes.'

'From choice?'

'No.'

'Then why do you have your own flat instead of sharing your parents' home?'

She gave him an agonised glance. 'Girls don't always want to be in the same place as their parents, do they?'

'Some do.'

She shrugged again and became silent and he wondered how much her loneliness came from her attempt to live like other girls, and how much because her parents preferred her out of their hair. She was an uninspiring sort of girl but it seemed to Pel that it would only require someone to be interested in her to change her enormously. He'd seen it happen before.

'Do you know where Madame Quermel goes?' he asked.

The girl's shoulders moved again. 'She's got some relations somewhere around. Perhaps she's got a fancy man as well. You know what widows are like.'

She seemed to sag in the chair again. She shot a frightened glance at Pel, as though worried she'd said too much, and he noticed she was watching Darcy with a desperate sort of look—as if, Pel thought, he were the last man in the world and she were the last woman. He suspected that she'd found her plain features and sallow skin a great drawback and that, instead of allowing her personality to develop to compensate for the drawbacks, had merely retreated into a shell of loneliness. He decided to let her go for the time being.

'I think I'll have a word with Madame Quermel now,' he said.

She looked faintly disappointed, as though she enjoyed men's company—any man's company—and was loathe to be put aside. 'Is that all?' she asked.

'For the time being,' Pel said. 'But I shall doubtless come back to you.'

Madame Quermel was small and well-shaped and, even if nervous, seemed in possession of herself, with a self-confidence and attractiveness that was entirely lacking in the girl.

'What do you know of Madame Chenandier?' Pel asked.

Madame Quermel shrugged. 'As much as anybody knows of the people they work for. In some things I knew a lot. In others, nothing at all.'

'Did she have men friends?'

She shrugged again. 'It's not my place to say.'

'To me it is.'

She hesitated. 'Well, yes,' she said. 'I think she did.'

'Lovers?'

'Why else would she have men friends?'

It was a point. 'Did anyone visit her yesterday?' Pel asked.

'I didn't see anyone.'

'What did she do?'

Madame Quermel considered. 'Much the same as she always did when Monsieur was in Paris. Got up late and spent a long time dressing. Then she went into the city. I'd asked for money for housekeeping and she said she'd have to go and get some from the bank. She stayed in the city for lunch and came back in the late afternoon, but I think she'd had some wine and she went up to her room and fell asleep. When I asked her for the money later on in the evening, she said her bag was upstairs but that she'd see I got it this morning.'

'She told you she'd drawn the money from the bank?'

'She said so.'

'She couldn't have given it to you and you'd forgotten?'

'I should hardly think so. They lived well and laid out a lot of money for food.'

'There was no money in her handbag,' Darcy pointed out. 'It was in the hall, open. There were about fifty frs, that's all.'

Madame Quermel shrugged. 'Then I don't know what she did with it,' she said. 'Unless she hid it among her clothes somewhere upstairs.'

'Check, Darcy.'

'Right, Patron.'

Pel turned again to the housekeeper. 'And last night?' he said. 'Did she entertain anybody?'

Madame Quermel gave another shrug. 'She might have done.'

'Don't you know?'

'My room's at the top of the house.'

'But you were in?'

'Yes.'

Pel paused for a moment. 'Odile said you were out,' he pointed out quietly.

She looked disconcerted for a moment, but she recovered quickly. 'I suppose she's been spying.'

'Is that what she does?'

'All the time.'

'Why?'

'I think she thinks I'm after her father.'

'Are you?'

'No, I'm not.' The answer came sharply, angrily. 'But she gets some funny ideas in her head. She probably wasn't even in.'

'She said she was writing letters.'

'Who to? She has no one to write letters to. No boy-friends. Hardly any girlfriends.'

'Why not?'

Madame Quermel shrugged. 'You've only to look at her.' The words were spoken with the contempt of an attractive woman for someone who was graceless, gauche and lacking in charm.

'And these letters she says she was writing?'

'She's always saying things like that. She's writing letters to her friends. She's meeting friends in the town. That sort of thing. It's all a pretence to hide the fact that no one shows any interest in her.'

Pel paused, thinking. Over the years he had developed a marked ability to judge characters and he'd suspected at once that Odile Chenandier's claim to be writing letters hadn't sounded quite honest. It would need checking.

He came back to his original line of questioning. 'But you,' he said. 'You did go out?'

'Not last night. The night before, I think. It's hard to remember.'

Pel's eyebrows rose. 'It's only one day ago, Madame.'

She gestured. 'A lot's happened, hasn't it? It's been a bit of a shock, all this. She must be getting the night before confused with last night.'

'She seemed quite certain. What *did* you do last night?'

'What do you mean?'

'Well, you just didn't sit in your room and stare at the walls, did you?'

She frowned. 'I watched television.'

'And saw what?'

'What do you mean?'

'I mean, what did you see on television?'

She frowned again. 'It was a film. Yes. A film. *L'Homme de Hong Kong*.'

'Sure?'

'Yes.'

'*L'Homme de Hong Kong* was three nights ago.' Pel happened to know because his housekeeper, Madame Routy, was a television addict and he'd been driven from the house and been obliged by the rain to take refuge in a bar. He'd enjoyed the bar about as much as he enjoyed television.

Madame Quermel was looking worried. 'Then I don't know,' she admitted. 'I always fall asleep, anyway, if I've had a tiring day.'

'Had you had a tiring day?'

'They're always tiring when Monsieur's away. She never likes—liked—being alone. She drinks—drank—a lot.'

'I don't think Madame's drinking was bothering you last night,' Pel said. 'I think you went out.'

'No! No!'

'What if Odile's prepared to swear? She's admitted she spies on you.'

She stared at him, on the point of tears.

'You did go out, didn't you?'

She nodded silently.

'Why didn't you say so?'

'A man tried to pick me up. I'm not used to men trying to pick me up.'

Pel wasn't so sure. 'Where?'

She hesitated before replying. 'On the way to St Antoine. I have relations there. It upset me. I had to run.'

'Did you report it to the police?'

'No.'

'Why not?'

'It was nothing. He didn't persist.'

Pel paused again to give her time to collect herself. 'When you came in, had you recovered by then?'

'Yes. Yes, I had.'

'So you'd be able to tell if there were anyone in?'

'I don't know.' She shook her head angrily. 'I didn't notice.'

'Were there lights on? Didn't you go and ask if there was anything Madame Chenandier wanted?'

'No. My evenings are my own. And I use the back door. I saw nothing and heard nothing. There must have been lights on in the hall, I suppose, so she must have been in somewhere.'

'Don't you know?'

'No.'

Pel frowned, irritated. Nobody ever seemed to keep their eyes open, he decided. As far as he could make out, the whole world except him went round with their eyes tightly shut. It was a wonder a few of them didn't get bloody noses from walking into closed doors.

'Didn't you notice *anything*?' he asked.

'No.'

With his own sensitive nostrils, it was beyond Pel why she hadn't *smelled* death in the house, but he supposed other people weren't so sensitive to smells as he was. Darcy often said they should put a collar on him and transfer him to the dog handlers.

'Didn't you hear music?' he asked.

'No.'

'Not at all?'

'No.'

'When did you hear about the murder?' he asked.

'From Odile this morning.' Madame Quermel gestured. 'When I came down, she was telephoning the police. I asked her why and she said "Take a look in the salon." I went, thinking there'd been a burglary or something. I came away and was sick. Then you came.'

'Didn't you hear anything that suggested something was happening?'

'I'm on the third floor and I sleep deeply. They'd have to drive a tank through for me to hear anything.'

'Do you have a suite up there?'

She gestured. 'Madame Chenandier liked to call it a

suite. It's a bedroom and a sitting-room with a bathroom along the corridor. If I want to make myself coffee, though, I have to come all the way down to the kitchen.'

Pel was silent for a moment, staring at his fingers, then he looked up. 'You said you were a widow, Madame,' he said. 'How long ago did your husband die?'

There was a long pause, and Pel noticed that the breeze had increased and was moving the trees outside so that the sun through them was moving in small spots on the floor. One of the policemen outside was obviously having a surreptitious drag at a cigarette, because he could smell the smoke, which had somehow been wafted through the window.

He repeated the question. 'How long, Madame?'

She stared at him, her eyes suddenly cold. 'What has that to do with this business?' she demanded.

Pel shrugged. 'Probably nothing,' he admitted. 'But it helps me to get to know the people who live here.'

She paused and he thought she wasn't going to answer. 'Four years ago,' she said at last. 'It was a road accident.'

'Did you get on well with him?'

'Yes.'

'And you had a normal relationship?'

'What do you mean by that?'

'I mean the sort of normal relationship that exists between two people who love each other.'

'Sexually? Is that what you mean?'

'Yes.'

She gave Pel an angry look. 'It was excellent,' she snapped.

'I see.' Pel nodded. 'I'm sorry to have to ask such personal questions. I hope you've got over it now.'

She frowned. 'Yes, I have. I had to.'

CHAPTER
THREE

The doctor had gone, and only the laboratory assistant remained with the fingerprint man, with his black and silver powders, dusting the doors, the windows, the piano and any surfaces likely to hold a print, blowing, studying with a magnifying glass and taking photographs.

Pel was wandering down the drive looking for bloodstains when Darcy reappeared downstairs.

'You'll not find any, Patron,' he said. 'I looked. The rain must have washed them away. It poured last night, remember.'

Pel said nothing and stared up the drive, past the house and down the gravel path into the garden. It was well laid out, English in style but French in upkeep, the lawns shaggy and the flower beds sparsely populated. The garage and two ivy-covered outhouses along one side ended up near the stream. One was a woodshed where a lawn-mower, tools and barrows were kept with two women's bicycles, the other a small box-like construction where Pel found a bench with small tools hanging on the wall. There was a Nicolas bottle, half-full of wine, *Le Bien Public*, the local newspaper, an empty Gauloise packet, a chair without a back covered with a sack, and crumbs from a baguette which indicated that it was where the gardener ate his mid-day meal. The walls were white-washed, with small pencilled notes scrawled on the one over the bench— obviously the gardener's reminders to himself about tasks he had to perform—a name or two, among which Pel identified a local seed-merchant, and a few telephone numbers. It covered a square metre of wall, and was clearly the result of years of scribbling memos.

Pel studied them all carefully, then he rubbed his nose and went into the house to find Prélat, the fingerprint expert.

'Anything?' he asked.

Prélat looked up. He was bald and thin-faced with rimless spectacles and looked like a professor. 'Nothing at all,' he said. 'Just prints belonging to the family. The housekeeper. The daughter. The husband. The murdered woman.'

'That all?'

'There are a few smudges that look like gloveprints, and two others we haven't yet identified, but I'm told there's a gardener and a brother who made a habit of calling.'

'What about the cars?'

'Same as the house. They belong to the owners and, by the look of them, they're the only ones who drove them. There are a few prints on the outside but those could have been done by garage-hands, passers-by or even the man in the moon. The steering-wheel prints belong to the people who owned them.'

Pel guiltily lit another cigarette and turned to Darcy. 'Find anything upstairs?'

Darcy looked exhausted. 'No, Patron. I checked every inch of the bedrooms. There's no sign of the money she drew.'

'Better find which bank she used and check that she actually did draw it,' Pel said.

He rubbed his nose again, drew on the Gauloise and went through the usual motions of a drowning man coming up for air. Darcy watched him with interest, as he always did. Despite his cynical attitude to Pel, he had a curious affection for him and enjoyed seeing him in action.

'What about the people next door?' Pel asked. 'Did they hear or see anything unusual during the night?'

'I haven't asked yet,' Darcy said. 'But why should they? She couldn't have been expecting anyone; you don't normally come down dressed in a see-through robe to answer the door. She was about to take a bath. The water's still in the tub, with a bottle of bath essence on the side. There's a nightdress laid out on the bed, too. That seems to fix the time of death pretty latish.'

Pel nodded. 'The gardener and that brother you mentioned: I thought you were getting hold of them.'

'I'm trying.'

'Try harder.'

'I never stop, Patron.' Darcy was unperturbed. He'd
been deflecting Pel's ill humour for so long it never even
touched him now. 'But it's not all that easy. They've both
disappeared. The brother lived in the village here but he's
not been seen this morning at all. The gardener's an Italian
who settled here with his sister in 1965. They both married
and the gardener was widowed. He lives in Bazay. I got the
local boys to enquire and it seems his landlady said he
wasn't in his lodgings last night or for breakfast this morning. His neighbours haven't seen him either.'

'They never have,' Pel muttered. 'I expect, like everybody else, they were going round with their eyes shut. Find
him. And while you're at it, check the housekeeper's
relations. She's supposed to have some in St Antoine. See if
she was with them when it happened. She says she was but I
don't believe her.'

He watched as Prélat packed up his bag and moved out of
the room to make an assault on the rest of the house. The
body was still on the floor. Pel grimaced.

The veins and arteries of a human being contain a
surprising amount of blood, but Camille-Jeanne Chenandier seemed to have possessed more than her fair share. It
was everywhere, sticking to the paintwork, smearing the
walls and doors, even splashing the ceiling, to dry sticky
and scarlet-black. The place seemed to have been decorated with it, and the sweet sickly smell assailed the nostrils.
Considering how much there was, it was incredible that
there were no fingerprints, no marks beyond smudges and
smears that seemed to indicate gloves.

'It makes you want to throw up, doesn't it?' Pel said. He
glanced at Darcy. 'If you were going to do someone in,
Darcy, how would you do it?'

'Not this way. Too messy. And too dangerous. You'd be
covered with blood. Whoever did this *must* have it all over
his clothes.'

'Or *her* clothes? It might have been a woman. What did
you think of the daughter?'

'Surly piece. Seems to have suffered a bit from neglect.'

'Did you ask her?'

'No, I asked the housekeeper.' Darcy smiled, his large white teeth flashing. He was a handsome young man and Pel knew he spent most of his time off duty popping in and out of bed with any pretty woman he could find. 'She's not bad,' he said.

'You've got the morals of a buck rabbit,' Pel growled. 'What did she say?'

'She said that the mother didn't get on with the girl.'

'Nothing unusual in that these days.'

'This was different.'

'How many ways of not getting on are there?' Pel raised his eyebrows. 'Check her clothes. All of them.'

'Right, Patron. Housekeeper, too?'

'Yes. But don't go at it like a lunatic. Use a bit of discretion. Just try to get them off her without an argument.'

Darcy grinned. 'I wouldn't mind, since you mention it,' he said. He pushed across a photograph. It showed an attractive dark-haired woman with good shoulders and a slender neck. It was not merely a formal photograph but a portrait designed to bring out the sitter's beauty to the utmost.

'Who's this?'

Darcy nodded at the body. 'Must have been quite spectacular in bed,' he said. 'It seems the daughter always regarded it as a personal tragedy that she didn't take after her.'

'Did the housekeeper tell you that, too?'

'Yes. There are a lot of other photographs like that in her boudoir upstairs. She seemed to fancy herself.'

'Probably had a lover somewhere,' Pel mused. 'Go on about the daughter.'

'Not clever. Bit sullen with her parents.'

'Aren't they all?'

'I'm not,' Darcy said. 'I'm the apple of their eye.' He pushed another photograph across. 'Seems she took after her father. That's him.'

Pel studied the photograph. It was an indifferent picture, and showed a man who was tall, strong-looking but far from handsome.

'Looks like a potato,' Pel said flatly. 'Ugly enough for an Englishman. Any more on the daughter?'

Darcy glanced at his notebook. 'She's always considered it a dirty trick that fate had her born looking like her father instead of like her mother. Seems it was obvious that was the way it was going to be even when she was small, and Mammy decided not to have any more in case they also took after Pappy.'

'Did the parents get on?'

Darcy shrugged. 'Nobody heard them quarrelling. But nobody saw them billing and cooing either.'

Pel turned and stared down at the body. 'Get rid of it,' he said shortly. 'Then let's go and have some lunch.' He sighed. 'I'm still ten years off my pension and when I've finished I'm going to grow tomatoes, stay in bed in the morning and eat at regular hours. In the meantime, I suppose I've got to endure. Come on.'

There were several reporters outside the house: Henriot, Pel noticed, from *Le Bien Public*; Fiabon, who represented *France Dimanche* and *Paris Soir*; and Sarrazin, who was a freelance and made Pel's life a misery ringing him up at night—usually when he was in bed.

'Anything to tell us, Inspector?' Sarrazin asked.

'Nothing you don't know already,' Pel said. 'Sergeant Darcy will give you name, place, time and anything else we have. Next of kin, religion, favourite flowers, nature of grandmother's rheumatism. I expect it all helps.'

'Who did it, Inspector?'

'I wish I knew.'

'Don't you have any suspicions?'

Pel shrugged. 'Not worth putting down on paper. We haven't been at it long enough. So don't go making guesses or I'll make sure you get nothing else.'

There was a little restaurant at the other end of the village, close to the school. Pel and Darcy sat on the terrasse over an apéritif and asked what was on the menu.

The proprietress didn't seem too sure. 'We've got some veal stew,' she said.

'That'll do,' Darcy said.

'On the other hand we've got some fish.'

Pel looked interested. Fish was good for a man with an indifferent stomach and he always felt *his* stomach was so indifferent it was a menace. 'I'll have the fish,' he said.

'Only,' the proprietress went on, 'it's gone off. Of course, there are tripes—' Pel looked hopeful '—but I think my husband's put his mark on them. He likes tripes.'

So do I, Pel thought wistfully.

In the end, they settled for the veal stew and it was brought out to them by the proprietress's daughter. She had good legs and a good waist but was hen-toed from wearing high heels, and had so much black make-up on her eyes the lashes kept sticking together.

'Did you ever see such a behind?' Darcy grinned.

Pel sipped his wine thoughtfully as he ate, thinking about Madame Quermel. *Her* waist was good, too, and her bust and behind were well rounded. Coldly, factually, he wondered if she was mixed up with whatever had been going on in the Chenandier household.

'That housekeeper,' he said, and he noticed that Darcy looked up interestedly. 'Think she had something going with Chenandier?'

Darcy gave a huge shrug that seemed to lift his shoulders to the level of his ears. 'She's got a good enough figure and a pretty enough face.'

'She's a widow, too. They sometimes miss what they've had, don't they?'

Darcy had his eye on the girl again. She was drinking a cup of coffee just inside the bar, making a noise like a fire hydrant every time she took a mouthful. 'I've always found widows more than eager,' he agreed.

'I expect you know,' Pel growled.

Darcy poked at his veal stew. 'Well, you know these lonely women. They have a habit of finding their way into a man's bed and, when they do, the least he can do is make them feel at home.'

Pel sniffed coldly. 'What else do you think about her?' he asked.

Darcy shrugged and smiled. 'Well, she's not very old,' he admitted. 'And it would be difficult *not* to notice her.'

'For you perhaps,' Pel said. 'What about upstairs? Anything missing?'

'Nothing I could see. Just the jewels the sergeant suggested. At least I didn't find any.'

'When did Chenandier leave for Paris?'

'Four days ago. It was a five-day visit. He went fairly regularly, it seems, selling wine to foreign exporters. He bought it in bulk and sold it in the north.'

'Cheap stuff?'

'It went mostly to London. In hogsheads.'

'I expect it was rubbish. The English aren't very fussy.' Pel sniffed at his stew. 'I think they took it from the pig bin,' he observed coldly. 'And I ought to have had Vittel water, not wine. Better for the inside. Make a check on Madame Chenandier, Darcy. See if she had a lover.'

'Think she did?'

'It's a guess. Women who have themselves photographed as often as she did usually have a high opinion of themselves. And women who have high opinions of themselves like to be admired.'

'Aren't we the philosopher?'

Pel looked up under his eyebrows. 'The trouble with you, Darcy,' he growled, 'is that you air your opinions too much. It'll do you no good. There are other sergeants in the office, you know, all itching to be transferred.'

Darcy set about his food without much worry. Everybody in the office—from the lowliest man on traffic duty— knew Pel, and most of them preferred to remain where they were, even if it were only directing traffic. He felt his job was quite secure.

CHAPTER
FOUR

The sun's heat seemed to intensify as the day drew out. The breeze dropped and, as the light took on the bronze colour of late afternoon, the temperature rose. Pel's temper rose with it because by this time he'd been on his feet all of eight solid relentless hours and they were hurting him. Besides which, because of the temperature, he'd had an extra beer after lunch and was convinced now that he was going to get indigestion. He hadn't got it yet but he firmly expected to before long and had even felt it wise to take a couple of bismuth tablets in case.

'Good for the stomach,' he explained to Darcy, making a mental resolve not to touch another drop until he was safely home and behind his own table.

When they returned to the house, the juge d'instruction had arrived to take a look at the scene of the crime. He was a young man called Brisard and new to the game. Pel had long since realised he was a little afraid of him and had been quick to take advantage of it.

'How are you getting on, Inspector?' Brisard asked uncertainly.

Pel shrugged.

'Will there be an arrest, do you think?'

Pel shrugged again and Brisard looked nervous.

'Are you moving fast enough?' he asked.

Pel looked coldly at him. Brisard was an unhealthy young man—tall but pear-shaped, with large hips and buttocks which gave his figure a curiously feminine line. He had an office in the Palais de Justice that was always full of flowers and photographs of his children, which Pel suspected were there more for show than anything else. He had little love for Brisard and never hesitated to show it.

'How fast am I expected to move?' he asked. 'I only arrived a few hours ago.'

Brisard tried to put things right. 'I understand your problems, of course, Inspector,' he said. 'I regret it if I appear to be chivvying you.'

Just try, Pel thought sourly.

'But you have to understand that I'm being chivvied in my turn by the Director of Prosecutions. He likes to get things moving.'

Pel gave his eloquent sniff, looking like a man pushed to the limits of endurance. Napoleon after Waterloo had looked the same. 'It's easy when you don't budge out of your office,' he observed.

The body had disappeared by this time, together with most of the technicians, and the house was silent. Odile Chenandier had vanished to her own flat and Madame Quermel was in the kitchen preparing herself a lunch of bread, tomato and cheese. She had a nervous look on her face, and seeing Pel watching her, she found him a bottle of beer.

'I don't feel like eating much,' she said. 'Not after what's happened.'

Pel nodded, thanked her for the beer and wandered off. The house was still, with the shutters drawn against the sun, and he paused at the bottom of the staircase, looking up, a frown on his face. There was a picture of Philip the Bold on the wall—a copy of one he'd seen in the Palais de Justice—and a series of miniatures, mostly of men in uniform dating from Napoleon through the period of the Franco-Prussian War. Judging by the blunt potato faces, he put them down as ancestors of Chenandier rather than his wife.

He frowned and began to prowl about the ground floor, staring at the furniture as if it might tell him a story; as if, almost, he were *demanding* that it tell him a story. Darcy was sitting at the desk in the study writing in his notebook and he looked up as Pel appeared. Pel was staring at the floor with such intensity he looked paralysed.

'What's up, Patron?' he asked. 'Disillusionment setting in?'

'Judge Brisard's been pestering me.'

'You don't like him, do you?'

'He has the soul of a pile of sand.'

Darcy grinned. 'I bet you sent him away feeling he'd been picked over and sorted out to within an inch of his life.'

Pel almost smiled and Darcy's grin grew wider.

'I bet you pulled the legs off flies when you were a boy, Chief,' he said.

'We need a few malcontents in this world,' Pel pointed out. 'What did Doctor Minet have to say?'

'The usual: Multiple injuries. Laceration of the brain. There'll be a report.'

'When did it happen?'

'He won't be precise. He says somewhere between ten p.m. and midnight.'

'What was she hit with?'

'Minet isn't prepared at this stage to be exact but he said it wasn't short and blunt like a hammer. He thought a long narrow weapon. Heavy, of course. Could have been a poker.'

Pel walked into the salon, carefully avoiding the bloodstains, and stopped by the fireplace. There were fire tongs, a shovel and a brush there, hanging on a four-hooked stand. The fourth hook was empty. Pel studied the stand for a moment then, using his handkerchief, he picked up the shovel and weighed it in his hand. It was of burnished steel and seemed as heavy as a girder.

'There's a poker missing here,' he said, returning to the study. 'It'll be a heavy one, too. Get someone out here and get him to set up a search for it in the stream and in those bushes on the other side. Whoever did her in might well have thrown it over.'

'Right, Patron, I'll attend to it. Who do you want? Nosjean?'

Pel shook his head. 'He'd probably get lost himself.'

'He gets around like a guided missile when he starts.'

Pel pulled a face. 'Try Lagé. He's a married man and growing fat. He'll take his time. It'll make for a better job.'

As Darcy disappeared towards the telephone, Pel lit a cigarette and moved throuoh the french window into the garden to smoke it. Studying the house, he drew in the smoke, wondering uneasily what it was doing to his lungs. Bending, he studied the paving by the french windows. There was a clear mark of dried blood there, and another, he saw, on the edge of the grass, as though someone had stepped in one of the puddles of blood just inside the door and tramped it outside.

'Leguyader!'

The lab technician's head appeared through an upstairs window. He was a small intense-looking man who resembled Pel even to the tart tongue.

'This blood outside? Is there any more?'

'Just that on the paving there, and a bit on the gravel and a mark on the grass. Apart from that, nothing.'

'What do you think?'

Leguyader took the same view as Darcy.

'That he went out that way, probably in a hurry—probably even running, so that he put his foot on the edge of the grass there—then went down the drive to the front entrance and into the lane.'

Pel studied the mark again. 'What did it? Boot? Wellington? Wader? Snowshoe?'

'Could have been anything. Naked foot or a golosh even. There's no clear print. I've had it photographed, but there'll be nothing.' Leguyader sounded almost pleased.

Pel straightened up and examined the door. There was no sign of a break-in but that was not unusual. So much had been written and spoken on television about how to get into a house with a spring lock, every burglar in France had perfected the technique. Even little boys knew how to do it and sometimes did. All the same, with Chenandier away in Paris, it was unusual that there'd been no bolts on the door, or a chain in place. But was it? Aigunay-le-Petit wasn't Paris or Marseilles. People living in country districts didn't expect burglars.

Though they sometimes got them.

Pel threw away his cigarette and stared round him. The stream that ran past the bottom of the garden had been made into a decorative pond, crudely built up with stones and flowers among the reeds. It hadn't turned out very well. The French were never very good gardeners. His own efforts looked like those of infants in arms on the beach at Royan, and even his lawn looked like the stubble in a wheat field.

He pushed his thoughts aside and concentrated on the stream. Beyond, in the distance, he could see the ground rising towards the high lands of the Doubs. Wondering if the intruder had come across the fields and into the garden that way, he found a rake and with the handle tested the depth of the water. At its deepest it was well over a metre and at its shallowest two-thirds of that depth, running over pebbles and large stones. The intruder couldn't have come that way, he decided, or there'd have been water in the house and wet prints. He felt the water with his hand. It was clear and icy cold and he guessed it came down from the hills.

He frowned as he wiped his fingers, and decided to visit the neighbours.

The next-door houses were both smaller than the Chenandier house, one of them old, the other modern and ugly. He tried the modern one first, and was shown by an elderly daily help into the lounge. He could hear children playing in the garden.

As the help disappeared, her place was taken by a small woman with dark eyes and hair, a plump woman with the look about her of a fat brown partridge. When he explained who he was and what he was doing, her large eyes became larger with shocked horror.

'I'm Madame Germain,' she said. 'Ernestine Germain. We've known the Chenandiers ever since we came here seven years ago.' She gave a nervous little smile. 'I say "known" but that's not really true, because I don't think Madame Chenandier approved of us building alongside them. Our house isn't quite as imposing as hers and I think she felt we destroyed the tone of the neighbourhood.'

'What about Monsieur Chenandier?'

'I think he was quite indifferent. He said "good morning" occasionally and once gave me a lift into the city when my car had broken down but for the most part he ignored us.'

She offered him a glass of wine and he was just about to shake his head when he changed his mind.

'A small one,' he condescended, uneasily remembering at the last moment his decision not to overload his stomach.

When it arrived, it was big enough to drown a cat in. Taking a wary sip, he looked up.

'What about your husband?' he asked. 'What did he think of Madame Chenandier?'

She smiled. 'He didn't like either of them very much. He makes plastic moulds and he has an office in Dijon and a small factory in Arles. He's away a lot down there. Everything he's got he's made himself with his own efforts and he hadn't much time for Monsieur Chenandier who started with inherited money and an inherited house; he had none at all for Madame Chenandier. Though it's awful to say it under the circumstances, he thought she was a snob.'

'Did you hear anything unusual last night?'

'No, nothing.' She paused. 'That is, I heard her playing opera at one point. Was that when it happened?'

'Yes,' Pel said. Murder set to music, he thought. Going out to Verdi's arias. Death to 'La donna è mobile.' 'What time would it be?'

'I didn't notice. Latish. I always heard her when she played the stereo. She liked to play it loud. She sometimes sang to the piano. My husband couldn't stand it and always used to slam the windows rather obviously.'

'Did you hear any cars last night? Anything like that?'

'No.'

'See anyone in the lane?'

'No.'

'See anything in the house next door?'

She indicated the window. 'If you look, you'll see we couldn't see anything even if we tried. The trees are in the way. Madame Chenandier even planted more when we first built the house, to stop us looking into her garden. It was like a notice saying "Keep out. Propriété privée." It's the

same from upstairs. You can't see a thing. You can't from
the Layes—the people on the other side.'

'You know the Layes well?'

She smiled. 'No. I was invited there when we first
arrived. But I didn't seem to fit in. We don't give parties or
play cards and our children are much younger. It was a
solitary visit—' she smiled again '—to be shown round the
house, I suspect. And then no more. We just didn't fall into
the pattern. I think the two families felt it was their lane and
rather resented it when we arrived.'

Pel paused, thinking. 'Did you ever see anybody going in
or out of the Chenandier house?'

'Only the housekeeper or the daughter. That is, apart
from the Chenandiers themselves. And there was a brother
and a gardener who came most days.'

'No others?'

'Only the tradesmen.'

'No—er—' Pel paused '—no single men, perhaps, who
made a habit of visiting during the day when Monsieur
Chenandier was out?'

Her eyes widened. 'You think she might have been that
sort?'

Pel frowned. 'I have no opinions at all yet,' he said. 'I'm
merely trying to find out.'

She gave a little tinkling laugh, as if she enjoyed scandal
at the expense of her superior neighbours. 'Well, I heard
stories in the village. The postman said he'd seen a man
there once or twice.'

'Did he know him?'

'No. He just saw a figure through the window.'

Pel nodded and, leaving, walked slowly down the lane to
the old house on the other side of the Chenandiers' man-
sion. Outside was a big grey Mercedes and he realised with
a shock that it was late enough in the day for the owner to
have come home from his office. The family were taking
apéritifs in the lounge—mother, father and two youngsters.

He introduced himself and was received with polite
curiosity and shown in.

'Drink?'

May God be merciful, Pel thought.

He was placed in a deep armchair and handed a Pernod. It was as imposing as Madame Germain's glass of wine.

'It's a big one,' he said nervously.

'Mustn't have people saying we're mean,' the man observed. 'I've no doubt you've had a tiring day.'

Much more of it, Pel thought, and he'd go home exuding the sweetness and light of a cat in a sack. 'A bit,' he admitted.

'I'm Laye,' the man went on. 'Gérard Laye. My wife, Hélène. My two children, Emile and Anne-Marie.'

Pel nodded and sipped at the drink, wondering how his stomach stood up to what it had to accept in the line of duty.

'I'm trying to find out,' he said, 'if anyone heard or saw anything last night. Any sounds? Any cars arriving?'

They shook their heads and Laye gestured. 'You can't see much from here,' he said. 'And they always kept themselves to themselves.'

Pel nodded and, glancing through the window, saw that the garden, though smaller than the Chenandiers', was much the same type, with the stream at the bottom beyond the lawn, and a view of fields at the other side of the willows.

He became aware of the family watching him, with a sort of wary dislike. Madame Laye was a handsome woman with an expressionless face and a tight mouth that seemed to indicate constant irritation, and he wondered what sort of dissensions tore at *this* family.

He opened his notebook. 'We'd better get the record straight, Monsieur,' he said. 'I'd better have all your names and so on.'

Laye's eyebrows rose. 'Are we suspects or something?'

'Of course not, Monsieur. But if my men need to ask more questions, it helps them find you more easily.'

Laye shrugged. 'You have our names. My children are students.'

'And you, Monsieur?'

'Engineer. We have an office in the city and a small factory on the Troyes road. We manufacture car accessories. Mirrors, fenders, hub caps. That sort of thing. We also have a small welding firm at Bazay, together with an office. It's not much. Two or three men. We've also got a garage on the Lyons road. Two brothers called Orbeaux who look after our vehicles and cars and do odd jobs for us. A few friends and neighbours use them, too. They're cheap and don't fuss.' He smiled. 'They're probably not very honest either, but that doesn't matter. They do what we want.'

'That the extent of your business interests, Monsieur?'

'No. I also have an interest in a car-hire group. It's a nationwide thing; we get so much competition from the Americans these days a lot of us got together and put money into it. We all run separate firms but they're all inter-connected. I have one here, one in Lille, one in Nantes, one in Lyons and one in Paris. I'm the major shareholder and what I say goes.'

'Names, Monsieur?'

'Here it's Action Autos. You'll know it, I expect. In Lille, it's Marc Ourgane Garages; in Nantes, Zip—that's all, just Zip; in Lyons, its Langrin Garages; in Paris, Luxe Cars. We hire them with or without drivers.'

'And you spend your time where, Monsieur?'

Laye shrugged. 'Moving about between them all. Sometimes here, sometimes there. Mostly here—in the city.'

'How well did you know the Chenandiers?'

Laye glanced at his wife. He was a big man, broad-shouldered and handsome, a good head taller than his wife.

'I didn't know them at all,' Madame Laye said. 'We were friendly, that's all.'

'I hardly exchanged a word with them,' Laye agreed. 'Chenandier was often away and Madame Chenandier kept very much to herself.'

The boy shook his head. The girl shook hers, too, almost too forcefully, then she rose. 'Excuse me,' she said, and left the room.

'Anything wrong, chérie?' Madame Laye asked.

'No.' The door closed and Laye smiled at Pel. 'Youngsters,' he said. 'They don't have much time for adults these days. Perhaps it's because you're a policeman. She's at the university and they don't seem to like the law at the university.'

Having more than once stood on the end of a line of uniformed men while students hurled chunks of paving stone at them, Pel was inclined to agree.

He addressed Madame Laye. 'Ever see any visitors during the day?' he asked.

She shook her head. 'No,' she said. 'I'm often out during the afternoons. My husband's at work and the children are at the university. I keep the afternoons for myself.'

'Doing what, Madame?'

She smiled at him. 'Playing bridge,' she said.

CHAPTER
FIVE

Pel was in a mellow mood when he reached home that evening. Having once started, it was hard to stop and he had taken a Pernod with Darcy and eaten an *omelette aux fines herbes* with tomatoes and a little chopped ham, which he'd felt would do his stomach no harm and probably settle all the drink he'd swallowed. The fact that he'd probably shortened his life by several years by the number of cigarettes he'd smoked didn't occur to him, and he was feeling in just the mood to relax with a little quiet reading.

Reading was a pleasure to Pel, and one of his chief joys were English thrillers. Somehow the English seemed to do them better than French writers and, with an older sister who'd married an Englishman at the end of the war, he'd often visited England and learned to speak and read English well—something that often stood him in good stead now that inflation had allowed the Americans to occupy Europe.

He was almost—but not quite—smiling as he opened the door. The house was depressingly small and, erected since the war when the art of construction had been set aside for quick profits, had walls that were paper-thin and contained a built-in soundbox. And at that moment the soundbox was shuddering to the noise coming from the only living-room the place possessed.

Pel's brows went down in a scowl. It seemed that Madame Routy was watching television.

As he appeared in the doorway, she looked up. 'Cowboy film,' she announced. 'Burt Lancaster.'

'It sounds like the siege of Paris,' Pel snorted.

She sniffed. 'I don't hear so well,' she said airily, turning back to glue her eyes once more on the galloping horses and the men in large-brimmed hats.

'You couldn't turn it down a little bit, could you?' Pel suggested, but she didn't seem to catch on. Perhaps, Pel thought, she not only didn't hear so well, she was actually stone deaf.

'After this it's a circus,' she said.

Pel's heart sank. 'You're going to watch the circus?'

'But of course!' Given a chance, Madame Routy would have watched television from getting up to going to bed. It was only during the period when she was doing the housework that Pel considered there was any peace in the house, and then he was usually in his office. 'After that there's a play. It's about the Free French in London during the war.'

'There'll be bombs?'

'Oh, I expect so.'

In desperation, Pel looked round for somewhere to sit down. Madame Routy was stretched on the settee with her feet in the only decent chair in the room—what Pel called *le confort anglais*—so that he had to side down in a French armchair that was notable chiefly for its hardness and the impossibility of finding any joy in its clutches. He stared desperately at the television.

'*Le gunfight,*' Madame Routy announced brightly, gesturing at the screen.

Pel glared savagely at Burt Lancaster, wishing to God someone would blow his head off so that there'd no longer be any point in watching the film or even in showing it. But it didn't work out that way. Burt Lancaster, as usual, came off best and, as they carried away his victim, Pel resigned himself to an evening of noise and chaos and an early departure to his bed—which, as it happened was situated directly above the television, so that he'd have to lie between the sheets, totally unable to read because every word from below would be audible, and quite unable to sleep for the same reason. It looked like being a dreary night.

During the evening, in desperation, Pel took refuge in a bar down the road. There was a television even there, blaring in the corner, so that the announcer made it difficult for him to concentrate on his beer.

'*Laborde s'avance. Il contrôle le ballon très facilement—*'

It was a football match between Reims and some Spanish team and everybody in the bar hung over the zinc counter, staring at the screen with their mouths open and their eyes out as if on sticks, listening to the blast as if they were all stone deaf.

'*A Roda, à Cevedola, à—mais non, Mathieu l'a pris—*'

Pel glared at the barman. 'How long does this go on?' he demanded bitterly.

'About another half-hour,' the barman said. 'It's a good match, isn't it?'

Pel thought it was murder. Brooding over the fact, he recalled that, all things being normal, he would have been looking forward to the week-end off. Everybody else had their week-ends off. Even Madame Routy.

He sat out the match, hoping for peace when it finished, but as soon as the football stopped, one of the young men who'd crowded the bar to watch, pushed a coin in the juke box and a pop group which seemed to be armed not merely with guitars and drums but also with bombs, cannon, rockets and a whole chorus of mad ferrets to give backing crashed out with the thunderous tumult of a dam breaking. Pel finished his beer in disgust and left.

It was only when he was in the street that he began to wonder if noise was one of the reasons why no one had heard anything unusual in the Chemin de Champ-Loups the previous night.

If Madame Chenandier had been playing grand opera on the stereo, it was probable she'd not heard the intruder enter, and equally probable that, if she were in, the house-keeper, used to the sound of music downstairs, had not really noticed it and had therefore probably not even heard anyone moving about. It might be a good idea, he thought, to pursue the idea the following morning, and he decided to ring Darcy.

He went back into the bar and asked for the telephone and a *jeton* to use it. Darcy answered and for a while Pel could hear scufflings and even whisperings and he decided in disgust that Darcy was probably in bed with a girl.

'Sure, Patron,' he said cheerfully when they'd sorted out who was to handle the instrument. 'I'll be there first thing. Waiting outside so that nobody nips away.'

Pel walked home in silence, deciding the world was a wicked place and that it was no wonder he spent half his life involved with crime.

When he got home, the television was still blaring out. He'd been right. The play about the Free French *did* include the blitz of London and he went to bed in a fury wondering how long it would be before he changed his role as detective for that of murderer, with Madame Routy as the victim.

It was only while he was brooding on Madame Routy's possible fate and the joy he'd have felt at being the ultimate director of her end that it occurred to him that no self-respecting burglar ever made a habit of entering a house where a record-player or stereo was playing music, whether it was pop, sentimental or operatic—at least not without doing a bit of checking first. It was one of the rules of the game. You even pulled the curtains and switched on the radio to discourage them.

So that—and he sat up in bed, for the moment unaware even of the crashings from the salon below—whoever had murdered Madame Chenandier could not have been a common or garden intruder but someone who was well aware of her predilection for making loud musical noises and was prepared to take advantage of it. Perhaps even someone who was well known to her, which would more than account for the absence of signs of breaking and entering.

The idea occupied his mind for so long, it was only when he decided to go to sleep that he realised that the bathroom taps were running and Madame Routy was in there, apparently—for she was a noisy individual even when she was being quiet—throwing toothglasses and nailbrushes at the wall, and that, blessed relief, the chaos downstairs had finally come to a halt.

Darcy was waiting in the Chemin de Champ-Loups the following morning when Pel arrived. He was smoking a cigarette and looking like a cat that had been at the cream.

Pel scowled at him, still occupied with thoughts of his ruined week-end. Darcy never seemed to get upset about extra work, taking his pleasures—usually women—where he found them, making no plans but always sufficiently well organised to be able to find entertainment when he needed it.

'Have a good night?' Pel asked sourly, remembering his tussle with Madame Routy.

Darcy grinned and moved the flat of his hand backward and forward. 'So-so,' he said.

'Blonde or brunette?'

'I'm a sucker for redheads.'

'You'll end up with a bad back and a worn-out prostate.'

Darcy grinned. 'What a beautiful death!'

'Who's on duty?'

'Everybody. Lagé, Misset, Krauss and Nosjean. Nosjean's bleating, of course. He had a date and he didn't fancy giving it up.'

'He'd better make up his mind whether he wants to be a detective or a traffic cop.'

Darcy grinned. 'He's just young. He hasn't learned yet to cope with the inroads it makes into his sex life. I checked with Estelle Quermel's relations at St Antoine, by the

way—an aunt and an uncle. She didn't go there. Nor would
I. They had the sort of faces that would curdle milk. They
don't approve of her.'

'Why not?'

'Chiefly, I gather, because they didn't approve of her
mother either. The whole family deployed themselves
round the room with me in the centre, while they told me
what they thought of her.'

'What *did* they think of her?'

'They think she's Chenandier's mistress, not his housekeeper.'

'It's an idea. Why did they think that?'

Darcy smiled. 'Only it seems because her mother
was some chap's mistress, too, and they felt it ran in the
family.'

'Is that all?'

'That was the only reason they could offer. When I
pointed out that she'd been married, they said, "Ah, but
she's not now. She's a widow." If you could like that lot,
you could like tarantulas.' Darcy paused and cocked a
thumb at the house. 'For your information, Patron,' he
ended, '*he's* back.'

'Who?'

'Chenandier. He arrived on an early train. He said he
saw about it in the papers.'

Pel stared through the window. It was a tranquil day, the
sort he'd always enjoyed in Vieilly where he'd grown up,
walking across the fields looking for trompettes de mort,
the shy black mushrooms that grew under the leaf mould at
the roots of trees along the edge of the woods. There were a
lot of afforestation areas at Vieilly and, thinking about it
now, remembering the winding road, the distant view of
the river and the long slopes of the Côte d'Or topped by
dark patches of trees, he wondered why he never saw it
these days.

'Do you want to see him, Patron?' Darcy asked, breaking
into his thoughts.

'Have you questioned him?'

'I reserved that pleasure for you, Patron. However, I did

check with the bank. She did draw that money all right: 3,000 frs.'

Pel frowned. 'Well, it wasn't in her handbag, was it? So where did it go?'

'The murderer?' Darcy suggested. 'He must have taken it, I expect that's what he was after and she interrupted him. That and the jewellery that's supposed to be missing. Find who's got those and you've got your man.'

Chenandier was in the hall, staring into the salon, across the door of which Darcy had fixed a tape the night before. He was a tall, well-built man, good-looking in a rude healthy sort of way that managed to impress without the advantage of correct features or fine eyes. His nose was shapeless and his hair colourless, but there was something about him—strength perhaps—that had a strong appeal. He was wearing a well-cut suit of a fine check, suede shoes and a spotless white shirt. In build and style he looked remarkably like Laye, his next-door neighbour. He'd apparently just arrived and his suitcase was still in the hall. He looked worried and uncertain and turned quickly as Pel appeared.

'I'm Hervé Chenandier,' he said. 'I've just got back.'

'Pel. Inspector Pel. I'm in charge of the inquiry.'

Chenandier gestured. 'This is a terrible thing, Inspector. She was only forty-three, and she was one of the most beautiful women I've ever known. She'd never have done anyone any harm. Why did they do it?'

His words tumbled over themselves as his thoughts spilled out, and as he spoke, he moved about the hall, clasping and unclasping his hands and beating the fist of one into the palm of the other.

'What in God's name happened, Inspector? Why should anyone do this to my wife? Was it some intruder she bumped into? It might have been, you know, because the house's full of things that could be stolen and I'm well enough known in the city here. People must have been aware of them. I read about it in last evening's paper in Paris. I came back as soon as I could.'

'What time would that be?' Pel asked.

'I caught a train at six o'clock this morning.'

Pel blinked. 'It must have been in the papers before that,' he pointed out.

Chenandier nodded agreement. 'It was,' he admitted. 'Last night. I just didn't see it. I was out on the town. I don't enjoy sitting in a hotel. I dined out and went to a show. When I came back, I got ready for bed and decided to read the paper before going to sleep. As soon as I saw the story, I rang for my bill and started to pack. I'd just missed the late night train, though, and had to wait on the station for the first morning train. I got in only an hour ago.' He gestured. 'This is awful, Inspector,' he went on agitatedly. 'Why did they do it? *Was* it an intruder? The paper said so.'

Pel shrugged. 'The papers always talk through a hole in their heads. So far, I don't know.' He glanced at Chenandier, deciding he was sufficiently in control of himself to be matter of fact. 'You realise, of course,' he went on, 'that I'll have to ask you a lot of questions?'

Chenandier stared for a moment. 'It hadn't occurred to me,' he admitted. 'Am I a suspect?'

'Everybody's suspect for the moment,' Pel admitted. 'Most will be eliminated pretty quickly, but, you understand, we have to ask questions and take statements if only to verify what other people say.'

'Yes, of course.' Chenandier seemed to accept the situation calmly. 'I suppose so. What do you want to know?'

'Your movements since you left here chiefly.'

'That's not hard.' Chenandier rubbed his forehead, thinking. 'I left on Monday morning.'

'How?'

'By car.'

'All the way to Paris?'

Chenandier grimaced. 'When I go to Paris,' he said, 'I prefer to go by train. Cars are nothing but a nuisance up there. I leave mine in the Rue Charles-Briffaut near the station, and pick it up on the way back. I've done it many times. I'm sure the attendant will remember it was there.'

Darcy caught Pel's look and made a note to check.

'Go on,' Pel said. 'About Paris.'

Chenandier gestured. 'I arrived in the afternoon. I dropped my bags at the hotel—'

'Which hotel?'

'Meurice. Avenue de l'Opéra. You can check, I'm sure. Then I did some business. I dined with my customer—I'm sure he'll remember—name of Croxley an Englishman with an office near the Meurice—and returned late to the hotel.'

'And Tuesday?'

'Business in the morning. Man called Chasse. Business lunch. I dined alone in the evening.'

'Proof, Monsieur?'

'I was in a restaurant in the Rue Jacob. La Plume Galante. I've been there before. They know me. I booked a table. Wednesday was much the same. I dined in the evening with a customer. Chap called Legendre. He has a business in the Rue Otéro. You can check with him.'

'What about Thursday, the night your wife was killed.'

'I did some business with a man called Coquibus. He's a wine exporter, Rue Jacques-Prud'hon. Thursday evening I dined alone. Friday morning I think I had breakfast in a bar. Coffee and croissants. I sometimes do if I get up early.'

'Let's go back to Thursday evening. Where did you dine?'

Chenandier frowned. 'I thought you'd ask, of course, but thinking about it, I find I can't remember, Inspector. Sometimes I like to walk and I just set off and dine where it takes my fancy.'

'Can't you remember the name of the restaurant?'

'I think it was in the Boule Mich'. Though it could have been St Germain-des-Près. I had a few drinks. I was feeling a bit low and went at the apéritifs a little too hard. I honestly don't have a clue. I remember walking away afterwards and finding myself in the Place St Michel before going back to my hotel. In the end I took in the show at the Bobino.'

'Were you with anyone who could verify that, Monsieur?'

Chenandier placed the torn-off half of a ticket on the

table. 'No,' he said. 'But I found that in my pocket and thought I'd better keep it to show you.'

'Why, Monsieur?'

'Why what?'

'Why did you think I'd want verification?'

'Well—' Chenandier gestured '—nobody wants to admit they think they'll be suspected, do they? It's a sort of private conceit, I suppose. It sounds like admitting guilt. But I knew it was within the bounds of possibility and I thought I'd better keep it.'

Pel rubbed his nose, wishing everybody would think as far ahead as Chenandier. 'And last night?' he asked in a flat voice.

'Last night I dined in the hotel restaurant and took in another show.'

'Another?'

'Yes. I go to the theatre a lot when I'm in Paris. It's better than sitting in a hotel room. I often go two nights running.'

'Where was it this time?'

'The Humeur.'

'Do you have proof? Another ticket perhaps?'

Chenandier placed the ticket on the table.

'Do you always save your theatre tickets?' Pel demanded.

'No.' Chenandier seemed agitated but as if he were trying hard to control himself. 'Like anyone else, I put them in my pocket in case there's any dispute about seats—as there sometimes can be—and I invariably find them several days later and throw them away. This time, of course, I *looked* for them. I was concerned that I'd been alone and had no alibi. Why, don't you believe me or something?'

'But of course, Monsieur. I was only curious.'

Chenandier was moving nervously about the hall again, straightening a picture, pulling a rug into place with his heel. Pel watched him.

'I would prefer that you touched nothing, Monsieur,' he said. 'One never knows.'

'Of course. Of course.' Chenandier gave him a quick nervous smile. 'I forgot. Clues, naturally. You have to look for clues.' He slammed his right fist into the palm of his left hand again. 'This is terrible, Inspector. I don't know what to say. I only learned what happened when I got back to the hotel.'

'What did you do? Telephone home?'

'I didn't think I needed to. I suspected at once that it was my wife.'

Pel studied Chenandier for a moment. 'Unusual, don't you think, Monsieur—not ringing?'

Chenandier shrugged.

'You suspected she was the victim of this murder you read about in the paper?'

Chenandier shrugged. 'The name was the same. The address was slightly wrong.'

'But you didn't think of ringing to check?'

'No, I didn't.'

'Why not?'

'Shock, perhaps. I don't know. I wish to God—' Chenandier stalked up the hall, turned, and came back quickly. 'What can we do?'

'We're doing all we can already, Monsieur,' Pel said. 'I'm afraid we're going to have to ask you for the clothes you had with you in Paris. We shall have to check them, of course. As we shall have to check everyone else's, too.'

'What for?'

'Traces of blood, Monsieur.'

'You don't think—?'

Pel gestured. 'I don't think anything,' he said. 'It's only a formality and I don't expect any problems. But, as you can imagine, as the dead woman's husband and since you weren't with anyone at the time, we have to consider you.'

'But I was in Paris!'

'We have only your word and two ticket stubs to confirm that at the moment. Eventually we shall be checking with all the people you said you met and with your hotel. It sounds as if there'll be no difficulty. But for the moment we must have your clothes.'

Chenandier looked worried. 'I hope to God this won't

get round the city,' he said. 'I'm well known there. It could affect my business.'

'We're very discreet.'

Chenandier gestured at the suitcase. 'Well, there's my bag,' he said. 'Anything I can do to help. There's a suit in it. I also had this one I'm wearing with me.'

'Coat, Monsieur? Mackintosh?'

'Just a grey plastic mac. It's in the case. It's one of those things you can put in your pocket. I don't believe in being in a rush like some businessmen, and if it rains I simply wait in a bar until it stops or I can call a cab.'

'What if it's cold?'

'I'm pretty tough.'

Pel nodded. 'I'll get Sergeant Darcy to collect your clothes,' he said.

'All of them?'

'Every one, Monsieur. Shoes as well.'

Chenandier stared nervously at Pel for a moment then he shrugged. 'I never realised before what it felt like to be a suspect in a murder case,' he said. 'Now I know.'

Pel spoke placatingly. 'You aren't suspected, Monsieur,' he pointed out. 'We're going through the motions of an enquiry and there are certain movements we have to make. This is one of them.'

'Have you questioned my wife's brother, Gervase Darcq?' Chenandier asked.

'Why do you ask that?'

Chenandier frowned. 'Because it's the sort of damned thing he would do.'

'Is it?'

'He's been nothing but a pest to me since I married. He's cost me a fortune one way and another. He's shiftless, crafty, cunning, dissolute, and most of the time penniless except when he's worked a wangle on some woman. He also has a temper. You should look him up.'

'I probably will eventually.'

'Why not now? You're questioning me. Why not him?'

Chenandier was suddenly growing irritable and Pel tried to calm him. 'One thing at a time, Monsieur.'

'I can't see why you haven't chased him up already?'

'I prefer to work my own way.'

'You don't know him. You should move.'

'I don't like to be hurried, Monsieur. If you'll change, Sergeant Darcy will come up to your room for your clothes.'

Chenandier studied Pel for a moment then he turned and headed for the stairs. A few minutes later Darcy reappeared with a suitcase.

'Pass it on to Leguyader,' Pel said. 'Tell Nosjean to handle it. Even his limited intelligence ought to be up to that. Then get hold of this brother who's missing. You have his name?'

'Yes, Chief. Darcq, Gervase Darcq.'

'Find him. Turn him up.'

As Darcy vanished, Pel went up the stairs. Chenandier was still adjusting his tie at the mirror in the bedroom. Pel indicated the wardrobe. Stacked in a compartment at the side were two squash rackets.

'You play squash, Monsieur?'

'Not now. I used to play a lot. I swam a lot, too.'

'No longer?'

Chenandier gave a little twisted smile. 'I'm getting a bit old now. But I've always been keen on keeping fit. I used to trot through the woods fairly regularly. Two or three miles. To get my weight down. It's very easy here. Straight out of the door and down the lane.' Chenandier gave his worried smile again. 'Then I came home with such an appetite, I always had an extra cup of coffee and two extra croissants. It didn't help much but I suppose I enjoyed it.'

'Do you still take this exercise?'

'No.' Chenandier gestured. 'It becomes more difficult as you get older to get out on a cold morning and start running. But it was a habit that died hard because I was always fit as a youngster. I did my military service with the paras.'

'North Africa?'

'Indo-China. Dien Bien Phu.'

'Prisoner?'

'Yes.'

'Any ill effects?'

Chenandier's yellow eyes were on Pel. 'Such as homicidal tendencies, Inspector?'

Pel frowned. 'I wasn't thinking of that.'

Chenandier's expression became more friendly. 'No,' he said. 'We weren't badly treated, in fact. There was enough food—just—and I managed to keep fit. They tried brainwashing us, of course, but I just thought about other things. About my business—or my father's, as it was in those days. I don't think I ever really noticed what they were saying. But, because I didn't object to it, they left me alone.'

Pel indicated the room. 'Is there anything missing that you've noticed, Monsieur?'

Chenandier peered in the wardrobe. 'I don't know. Madame Quermel checks my clothes. You'd have to ask her.'

'Not your wife?'

Chenandier shook his head. 'Not for a long time, Inspector. She left it to the housekeeper.'

Pel nodded. 'What about valuables?'

Chenandier glanced about him. 'Well, I've not had a chance to check yet, but my wife did have some jewels.' He moved to an open drawer. 'She kept them here, I think.'

'You don't seem very sure.'

Chenandier blinked, then he seemed to shake his head as though to rid himself of some unpleasant thought. 'When I—when—' he stopped and drew a deep breath. 'I didn't use this room except for my clothes, Inspector. I sleep in the dressing-room next door, and have done for some time.'

'Can you give me a date?'

Chenandier's shoulders lifted. 'Hard to say. Three years? Four? About that.'

'And why, Monsieur?'

'Why what?'

'Why sleep apart from your wife?'

Chenandier shrugged and gave his small worried smile again. 'Well, you know how it is, Inspector. As you grow older you think more of sleep than the other thing. Besides, like most men, I snore, and my wife said it kept her awake. It made no difference to us.' He paused. 'In fact, I think it made things better because she was happier and got more sleep. Do you understand?'

Not having married, Pel didn't, but he nodded.

Chenandier drew a deep breath and, when Pel didn't pursue his questioning, he seemed to shake himself as though to drive away the events of the morning. 'Well, if there's nothing more you want—?'

'Not at the moment,' Pel said.

'But there might be later?'

'That depends.'

'On what?'

'On what we find out.'

'About me?'

Pel shrugged. 'Or about other people,' he said.

CHAPTER
SIX

The temperature increased, shooting up suddenly so that the hot air hung over the city like a suffocating blanket. The place gasped and between the tall tenements, the streets seemed to boil. The Place des Ducs wavered in the shimmering heat that rose from the traffic, while the Hôtel de Police appeared to be specially designed to trap the sunshine, and its occupants looked longingly at the people sitting behind their bocks of beer on the terrasse of the café opposite. The week before, everybody had been complaining about the lack of sunshine. Now they were complaining it was too hot.

Pel loved it, feeling it went a long way towards staving off his increasing rheumatism. Since Madame Routy had warned him she was going to visit her sister, he dined in the city, eating coq au vin in the open air near the Place du

Théatre. He was still in a good mood when he reached home, fully intending to take advantage of the absence of television noises, and he was just sipping a glass of wine in a chair in the garden when Darcy rang to say that Madame Chenandier's brother had been turned up at Jailly-les-Moulineux, staying with his landlady's cousin.

'They have something going,' he said, 'and the landlady doesn't approve. I'm not surprised, either. He was very drunk and very difficult.'

'Where is he now?'

'He tried swinging his fists, Patron, so I brought him in to let him cool down. It seemed a good idea. The uproar was like Versailles at the birth of a dauphin.'

'Right,' Pel said. 'See what you can get from him, then let him sweat it out. I'll see him in the morning.'

That at least was a step in the right direction, he thought, and prepared to enjoy his evening. But he was just stretched out on the settee with a book in a glow of well-being, a second glass of wine alongside him, when a car drew up outside and Judge Brisard appeared on the doorstep to find out what was happening. He hedged all round the subject in an attempt to dig out of Pel some facts without appearing to, and irritated, Pel produced cigarettes and a bottle of marc and they chatted for a long time about Brisard's health, even for a while in accord because Brisard seemed to suffer from the same horror of ill health and old age that Pel did.

When they got on to the Chenandier case, though, it was different, with Brisard fidgeting about as if he needed to go to the lavatory. Listening doggedly, Pel seethed inside, wondering why the man hadn't the courage to come out with it and say what he meant.

Eventually they got down to facts but, as Pel could have announced half an hour before, there was nothing to report. The people at the top always gave themselves headaches wondering why the men on the spot weren't making progress when, in fact, they were. As they always did—slowly, patiently, edging forward inch by inch, getting rid of the unnecessary details first and linking up all the

connecting ones. For some reason best known to themselves, examining magistrates always seemed to expect all
detectives to be Maigrets, when they ought to have known
from sheer experience that police work was more often
than not a simple process of elimination after a long period
of checking and cross-checking by a great many policemen
standing, as Pel so often did, on their own two weary flat
feet.

Brisard got nowhere and in the end changed the subject
in sheer desperatioin. 'That railwayman, Giulle, who was
found shot,' he said. 'What progress have you made there?'

'Not much,' Pel admitted.

'Was it suicide?'

'I don't know,' Pel said. 'We're looking into it. It *looked*
like suicide because it was his own gun and it was alongside
him with his fingerprints all over it. But I'd like to know
more about it first.'

'And what are you doing about it?'

'Talking to everybody in Marsonnay who might know.
I've got a man on it. But even the chap next door—chap
called Roger Barbièry who works at the enquiry desk at the
station—couldn't help. He was the one who found him and
reported it to Incidents.'

'Couldn't he tell you *anything*?'

Pel frowned. 'He bored me stiff most of the time talking
about railway time-tables,' he said. 'He knows them for-
wards, backwards and inside out. He's obsessed with 'em.
He's one of these chaps who buys them for light reading and
spends his spare time working out how to get to Toulouse
from Arles via Paris and gain ten minutes on the direct
route.'

Brisard frowned. 'I can never tell whether you're joking
or not, Inspector,' he said.

Pel shrugged. 'Neither can I,' he admitted.

Glad to see the back of Judge Brisard, Pel rushed back to
the settee. Putting his feet up, he relaxed happily once
more, hoping to get in some reading, but, to his disgust, he
fell asleep instead and woke up at 11.00 p.m. with a sour

mouth just in time to stumble to bed, and was just in a deep sleep at midnight when a thunderous roar beneath him announced that Madame Routy had returned from her sister's and had decided to watch the late film.

The evening which had promised so well had turned out a disaster.

He woke too early, feeling brown and crinkled round the edges like the first leaves of autumn. His bedroom had been stuffy in the heat, and his good humour when he arrived at the office was in an advanced state of disrepair. He put it all down to his health and advancing age and helped himself to a couple of bismuth tablets. Not that they ever did much good, he thought bitterly. Despite the claims that were made for them, all they did for Pel was leave a chalky taste in his mouth.

He was just glaring at the doodles on his blotter when Darcy arrived. He looked cheerful and Pel disliked him at once. No one had a right to look as cheerful as Darcy always did.

'Well?' he asked. 'Done a check on all the vagrants, tramps and other assorted drop-outs who might have done in the Chenandier woman for a spot of ready cash?'

Darcy didn't turn a hair. 'It's being done now, Patron.'

Pel frowned. 'Better also have a look at all known alcoholics and drug addicts in case they were after her money to buy themselves a bottle or a fix. Any known nuts?'

'Only Barbièry, the chap who lives next to that railway-man, Giulle. He's a nut.'

'Only on railway timetables. You needn't bother with him. What about the brother?'

'Still sweating it out downstairs, Patron. He'd been hitting the bottle pretty hard and he looks like something the cat dragged in. It wasn't very clever of him to go and stay with his landlady's cousin in Jailly, was it?'

'Perhaps he isn't a man who's full of good ideas. What about that Italian gardener? Has he turned up yet?'

'Not yet. But I've found out that he has a record. Madame Quermel let it slip.'

'When?'

'She gave me a beer.'

'Where?'

'In the kitchen.'

'As a prelude to further advances on your part, no doubt.'

Darcy grinned. 'You know me, Patron—'

'Only too well. Keep your nose clean, Darcy. What did she say?'

'Apparently he once confided in her when she was giving him coffee. I looked him up. Two cases of fraud, three of stealing from parked cars, one of assault, one of attempted blackmail.'

'You'd better make enquiries about him.'

'Where, Patron?'

'He must have relatives. He married a French girl. For all we know, he was probably related to Mussolini or someone. Go and ask them. And while you're at it, let's have all those cars checked for blood. Odile's. Quermel's. Chenandier's. Even Laye's. You never know. With all the blood that was splashed around, there ought to be some somewhere.'

'I'm pretty busy, Patron? Can't Nosjean handle it?'

'Nosjean's checking the land beyond the stream for the weapon. The Proc wanted Lagé for something of his own, and Krauss is off sick.'

'Misset then?'

'He's handling the Giulle death. His wife's expecting a baby and he wants to be free when it comes. I decided Misset could drop that better than anything else. That only left Nosjean.'

'He's got a couple of uniformed men out there to do the work for him.'

Pel shook his head. 'With the capacity for mental calculation that Nosjean possesses, if he had to do two things at once he'd make a mess of both of them. He's all right for answering the telephone and putting reports in the right files. After that—well, after that, he's good for fetching the coffee or a bottle of beer on a hot afternoon. He'd get himself in a knot. He has an unparalleled virtuosity for getting himself in a knot.' Pel dismissed the subject with a wave of his hand. 'Got the doctor's report yet?'

'Unofficially, Patron. Just what we expected. Lacerations to the brain. All the usual. In blunt terms she's dead because somebody hammered her head flat. Nothing else. No signs of recent sex. It's being sent along.'

'How about the lab report?'

'Much the same. Nothing unexpected.'

Pel scowled. 'We're getting along fast, aren't we?' he said.

As the door closed behind Darcy, Pel lit a cigarette, spat out a few fragments of tobacco, wondered—with all the bad habits he possessed—how many more years he had to live, and began to study the piles of paper on his desk. Without thinking he began to doodle again on his pad.

'Suspects,' he wrote. 'Hervé.' He crossed it out and wrote 'Chenandier'. Then he wrote 'Quermel. Odile. Gardener—when he turns up. Gervase Darcq, brother.' Then he wrote 'Neighbours—Layes and Germains,' underlined it, put a row of question marks after it, drew a square round it and added frills. It didn't tell him much and he'd already virtually written off the Germains because, as comparative newcomers, they'd never really been assimilated into the set-up in the Chemin de Champ-Loups, and Madame Germain appeared to have spent a lot of time with her mother at St Seine-l'Abbaye, to the north of the city, while her husband seemed to be perpetually away in Arles.

It still left Madame Quermel, Odile, the gardener, Darcq, Chenandier himself—if he'd somehow arrived from Paris, which seemed unlikely—and the Layes next door. He studied the sheet of paper, drew a few more frills round what he'd written, then he screwed it up and threw it in disgust into the waste-paper basket, and lit another cigarette from the old one, with a sigh at his own lack of will.

The door opened and Darcy appeared. 'You'd never believe it, Patron,' he said. 'While we've been slandering

Nosjean he's been pulling off a feat of detection. It seems he got in touch with the leader of the Italian community in the city. There's a small one, as you know. They knew of that sister the gardener had. And that's where he'd moved to. She lives in Boux. Nosjean apparently telephoned the police there. On his own. Without any help from anyone.' Darcy grinned. 'Only one problem.'

'Which is?'

'He isn't there at the moment. He's here somewhere—in the city. The sister said he went out on his motobicyclette.'

Pel scowled. 'What sort of report is that supposed to be?'

Darcy smiled. 'Just thought you'd like to know that Nosjean's not entirely a fool. He may actually have possibilities. Apparently he even alerted the uniformed boys.' He gave Pel a quizzical look. 'You look under the weather, Chief. You all right?'

'I didn't sleep.'

'Try a sleeping pill.'

'It would need an anaesthetist to overcome the racket my housekeeper makes.'

'What's she do? Throw parties in the kitchen?'

'She plays the television.'

'All the time?'

'From the children's shows in the morning to the late film at night. Particularly the late film at night.'

Darcy grinned. 'You should sack her,' he suggested.

'Who'd look after me?'

'There must be some plump young woman who'd give her right arm to share a house with Detective Inspector Evariste Clovis Désiré Pel.'

Pel glared. 'Are you trying to be funny?'

'No, Patron. But you're not old. You're a catch.'

Pel began to look nervous. 'I'll stick to Mother Routy,' he said. 'She's not a bad cook. She just goes mad with the television.'

'Perhaps you should marry her and whip her into bed. That would keep her quiet. It usually does.'

'You've got a one-track mind, Darcy.' Pel stood up. 'Let's have a talk with Madame's brother. Fetch him in.'

Gervase Darcq was a big shambling man with a face like an unmade bed—ravaged with drink, florid, fleshy and with pouches under his eyes big enough to stuff a suit in.

He sat down opposite Pel, flopping heavily into the chair. He held up a cigarette and raised his eyebrows.

Pel waved. 'Go ahead.'

Darcq lit the cigarette, drew in smoke as if his life depended on it, and looked at Pel.

'Am I a suspect?' he asked.

Pel shrugged. 'At the moment, no.'

Darcq sighed, as if in relief, opened and shut his jaws once or twice as if his tongue was clove to the roof of his mouth.

'Merde alors!' he said. 'Last night! Comme j'étais bourré. I was stoned. My head's like a dogfight and, Mother of God, how I suffer!'

He shifted inside his clothes, which were unwholesome with spots of drink and food. He turned and stared about him, squinted at the sun coming in through the window, turning his head away as if the brightness hurt his eyes, and began to open and shut his mouth again.

'That sun,' he said. 'It comes at you like a mad dog!'

'Try drinking less,' Pel suggested.

Darcq gave a sheepish grin. 'Unfortunately, booze comes at you like a mad dog, too. At least, it does me. Come to that, so do the women. Perhaps I'm just weak-willed.'

He gestured at the room. 'You sure I'm not a suspect?'

'I'm sure.'

'Why am I here then?'

'Because we've got some questions to ask you?'

'Because you think I did it?'

'Did what?'

'Bash my sister's head in. I saw it in the paper. I bet you think I did.'

'Bolting didn't discourage the idea. *Did* you?'

'No.' The big man shifted in the hard chair. 'But I got the wind up.'

'Why?'

'Because I was always fighting with her. She got too big for her boots. We were just ordinary people. My father kept a shoe shop. When she married Chenandier, she started thinking she was someone important. She didn't like me around.'

'Why not?'

The big face stared at Pel, then it suddenly lit up with a smile that would have charmed the ducks off the water, and Pel saw what it was that made for Gervase Darcq's success with women.

'She thought I'd pinch the television set or something.'

'Would you?'

'Wouldn't have minded. It would have brought in a few francs.'

'Did you ever take anything from her?'

'Few things. Not much. Helped myself to some of her brandy once. Borrowed her car when she wasn't looking. Used her name to get some clothes I needed.' Darcq paused. 'Forged a cheque in her name once. I did a couple of months for that because her husband found out and, being the mean bastard with money that he is, he insisted on her taking action. That was what finally finished her off. She told me I wasn't to go near the house any more.'

'And did you?'

'Of course I did.' Darcq grinned. 'I was her little brother, wasn't I? And she'd been responsible for me ever since my mother died. She still kept slipping me a few francs in spite of her husband. Not much, but a few. She hated it. She hated me, too. I suppose I can't blame her.' He paused and looked at Pel. 'Did Chenandier do it?'

'Do what?'

'Bash her head in?'

'Why should he?'

'Because he's a hypocritical bastard.'

'Oh? How?'

'The way he behaves.'

'How does he behave?'

'You'd think he was a saint.'

'And isn't he?'

'No, he isn't.'

'What does he do?'

Darcq shrugged. 'Merde, I don't know! I expect he gets up to all sorts of things when he's in Paris.'

'Do you know this?'

'No. But it's obvious.'

'That's a dangerous thing to say without proof.'

'No man's that good.'

'It doesn't pay to judge people by your standards.'

'You taking his side?'

'No. What makes you think he got up to things in Paris?'

'Oh, God!' Darcq waved a fleshy paw. 'I don't know. If you want proof, I haven't any. It's just a feeling, that's all.'

Pel studied the big man for a while. 'Where do you work?' he asked.

'FPSM. They've got a branch here in the city.'

'Doing what?'

'Machinist. We make tractor parts.'

'What about the night of the murder? Where were you?'

Darcq grinned. 'Bar de la Frontière,' he said. 'I usually am. And I was broke. That's normal, too. I expect someone else paid. Some girl, I suppose.'

'Which girl?'

Darcq grinned again. 'I haven't the foggiest. That's one thing about the way I get drunk. I can never remember afterwards so I never have to apologise or thank anybody. If they leave the bed before you wake up, how can you?'

Pel paused, taking a long time to light a cigarette to let Darcq stew in his own juice. After a minute or so the big man began to fidget and finally, he stubbed out his own cigarette and cadged another from Pel. Pel sat up.

'Chenandier,' he said. 'Your brother-in-law: Did he have any reason to want your sister dead? Money, for instance?'

'No, it was all his.'

'Women?'

'Well, there was that housekeeper of his. Quermel. I should think she's good in bed.'

'Was he having an affair with her?'

Darcq shrugged. 'I'd have loved to have caught them at

it. It would have been worth a few francs to me to keep quiet. It might even have been worth a few francs from my sister, too, not to tell the neighbours. But I never did.'

'Did you have reason to *suspect* they were having an affair?'

'Only that she was *worth* pushing into bed and Hervé Chenandier was a bit of a bull for women.'

'Was he?'

'I've told you. Ask him what he got up to in Paris. It wasn't all business, I bet.'

'You don't like him?'

'He's not exactly a fan of mine either. I expect he was the one. Are you going to let me go?'

'Yes. If I can rely on you not to disappear again.'

Darcq gestured. 'I promise. I'll stay home and be a good boy.'

'We'll also need to check your rooms and your clothes.'

'What for?'

'It's a formality.'

'If you're looking for blood on them, you won't find any.'

Pel shrugged and Darcq grinned. 'What do I do in the meantime? I've only got what I stand up in.'

'I expect we can lend you a blanket.' Pel turned away, then he paused. 'You'll be charged, of course.'

'With murder?'

'With assaulting the police last night.'

Darcq's look of shock turned to one of indignation. 'I didn't touch the police.'

'You had a good try.'

When Darcq had gone, Pel sat staring at his papers for a while, flicking through the reports he'd received. So far, there wasn't enough to suggest anything worthwhile, and in the end he ordered a car and drove out to Aigunay-le-Petit where he found Sergeant Nosjean at work, his youthful face pink. As he greeted Pel with his usual wary manner—as if he expected Pel to attack at once—Pel noticed Odile Chenandier's back vanishing round the side of the house.

'What's she want?' he asked.

'Nothing, Chief.' Nosjean looked embarrased.

'Has she been asking you anything?'

'No, Patron.' Nosjean blushed again. 'She just seemed to want to talk, that's all.'

'What about?'

'Me. What was it like being a policeman? Was I married? Did I have a girl? She got in the way a bit.'

'In the way of what?'

'Well, I found something, Chief.'

'Go on,' Pel encouraged. 'Tell me.'

'We've checked that land beyond the stream, Patron, and we found a half brandy bottle.'

'What's a half brandy bottle? A bottle half filled with brandy; a bottle containing a mixture half brandy, half water; half of a broken bottle which once contained brandy, or an empty bottle, half measure, which once held brandy.'

'That.'

'WHICH?'

'An empty bottle, half-litre size, bearing a label marked Les Quatre Ducs Cognac. Three star. It's not an old one. There's even a drop left in it.'

'Thank you,' Pel said coldly. 'When I get reports, I want them factual and in such a way they leave me in no doubt. What else?'

'Not much, Patron.' Nosjean's pinkness this time came from humiliation. 'A cigarette end or two. One right in the middle of the back lawn. A Gauloise.'

Pel eyed him speculatively. 'And what do you deduce from that?' he asked.

'That the murderer was probably someone who enjoyed smoking Gauloises.'

Pel's expression was pitying. 'There are around 52,000,000 people in France,' he said slowly and patiently. 'Out of those, including the kids who shouldn't be smoking but do, perhaps 25,000,000 smoke Gauloises. It certainly could have been the murderer's, as you so succinctly suggest, but on the other hand, it could also have belonged to the gardener, the dustman, the man who came to paint the house, the man who attends to the telephone, the house-keeper, or one of your own men. It could even have been tossed out of an aeroplane on a routine trip from Paris to Monaco. In point of fact—' Pel drew a deep, sad, disillusioned breath '—it's mine. I threw it down yesterday.'

As Pel turned away, he saw Darcy watching him, a grin on his face. 'We've done a check on what jewellery's missing, Patron,' he said.

'And what *is* missing?'

Darcy opened his notebook. 'A ruby ring worth quite a bit of money, for a start. There was also a diamond and sapphire ring and two diamond rings. Worth quite a packet altogether. Some other things as well. I have a rough list.'

'Where were they usually kept?'

'In the bedroom. In that open drawer.'

'Anyone know where they were?'

'Perhaps.' Darcy shrugged. 'Perhaps everybody. There were other things to take as well. There's a clock there worth a lot that would fit in a pocket, and a fur worth a franc or two.'

Pel seemed unimpressed. 'Did you check the clothes of those two women?' he asked.

'Yes, Patron.'

'Find anything?'

Darcy grinned. 'Chiefly that Quermel has a very sexy line in underwear.'

'You're developing into a fetishist. Any signs of blood?'

'Not on hers.'

Pel turned. 'And the daughter?'

'On the sole of one of her shoes. I gather it was the pair she was wearing when she found her mother. It's possible, of course that she picked it up when she went into the room.'

'She told us she *didn't* go into the room.' Pel said. 'She could see the corpse from the doorway. So why go into the room?'

Darcy smiled. '*She's* probably a fetishist too.'

CHAPTER
SEVEN

When Pel left the Hôtel de Police at the end of the day, Nosjean was sulking in the outer office. There was no doubt of his disapproval. You could as easily have remained ignorant of an escape of gas.

He watched as Pel vanished. 'The way that man behaves to me,' he said with the bitter gloom of a young man whose life had been blighted, 'you'd think he was thinking of raffling me off as a prize.'

'Since you mention it,' Darcy said, 'it's not a bad idea.'

Unaware of the passions he'd stirred up, Pel drove home slowly. Down the Rue Chabot-Charny, by the Place Wilson and out towards the University. His car was giving trouble, so he left it at the garage for a check, promising to pick it up the following morning. Then, lighting a cigarette, he began to climb up the Rue Martin-de-Noinville towards his home.

As he stopped, he was puffing and, deciding he'd mislaid a lung somewhere, made up his mind for the ten thousandth time that he'd have to cut down his smoking. But the first sight of his home shook him so much he lit another at once without thinking. It was desperately in need of paint and looked far worse than any of the others in the road. It looked, in fact, like a load of old doors and windows just dumped down at the side of the road, and he realised it was because his neighbours—shop-owners, managers and junior executives to a man—not only had more money than he did but also had more time at their disposal.

He opened the door with a sigh and instantly became aware of a small boy in the lounge watching television with Madame Routy.

'This is my nephew, Didier Darras,' she announced. 'My sister's had to go and look after her father-in-law so he's come to stay a day or two with me. He can have the spare room. It'll be all right, I suppose?'

Pel scowled. 'Just behave as if the place were your own,' he said.

His sarcasm went astray and Madame Routy nodded, her eyes still glued to the television. 'Thanks,' she said. 'I thought it'd be all right.'

The boy looked at Pel and smiled. It was such a wide smile, such a real one, and of such charm, that even Pel's hard heart melted.

'Does *he* like television, too?' he asked anxiously.

'Yes,' Madame Routy said.

'No,' Didier Darras corrected at once.

Madame Routy tore her eyes away from a talk on the cathedrals of France which, judging by the noise the volume control was causing, could easily have been on the storming of the Bastille. 'But of course you do,' she said.

The boy frowned. 'No, I don't,' he said.

'Surely you like *les cowboys*? *Le gunfight*?'

'No, I don't. Anybody knows that cowboys must have been a dirty, smelly lot who never shaved. On the television they look like a bunch of aunties.'

'Aunties?' Pel said.

'Homos.'

Madame Routy turned, frowning, and the boy made things clear. 'Homosexuals,' he said.

'You shouldn't know about such things,' Madame Routy said.

'Everybody else does.'

'You should watch the cowboys.'

'I might if they *looked* like cowboys.'

Madame Routy seemed to be on the retreat. She gave Didier Darras a dirty look. Almost as if he were allying himself with Pel. 'You seem to know a lot about it,' she said tartly.

The boy nodded. 'I do. I read it in a history of the Wild West. Got it for my birthday. 480 pages. With pictures. You should have seen Annie Oakley. She was on a horse. It was hard to tell which was which.'

Pel was listening to the exchange with something akin to delight. He thought he might have found a friend.

'Interested in gardening?' he asked the boy.

Didier shrugged. 'Not much,' he said. 'But it'll be better than television.'

They went outside to the minute plot behind the house where Pel endeavoured entirely unsuccessfully to grow vegetables and flowers.

'You a flic?' the boy asked.

'I suppose you'd call me that,' Pel agreed.

'F.L.I.C.' The boy grinned. '*Fédération Lamentable des Imbeciles Casqués.*'

'Is that what they think about us?'

'I don't suppose it's true.' The boy studied the wilting marigolds. 'They don't do very well, do they?' he said.

Pel shrugged. 'I only grow them to give me an excuse to get away from the television,' he admitted. A horrible thought occurred to him. Perhaps this child had worse habits than television addiction. 'If you don't watch television,' he said, 'what *do* you do with yourself?'

'I play boules.'

'Any good at it?'

'Not very. But I like it.'

'I've got a set,' Pel pointed out. 'Let's have a game.'

Jules-Pierre Leguyader, head of the Laboratory and Forensic Science Department, had no great opinion of his fellow men. According to Darcy, he much preferred the corpses he dealt with and, among the denizens of the Hôtel de Police he had a habit of stirring things up just to show how much he disapproved of them.

The real cause, in fact, was that he was a painstaking man and considered that other men just didn't bother enough, whether it was the detective presenting him and his laboratory with things to check or the grocer in the corner épicerie who couldn't be bothered to stack his vegetables properly. Sometimes, Leguyader's care for detail gave him indigestion and it certainly never improved his temper.

The sun was streaming through the window on to his bench, turning golden-bronze now as the evening came. About him the lab was silent because everybody had gone home except Leguyader, who was staring at the clothing spread in front of him with a very real distaste.

At least it was clean, he thought, which was something. It was one of the hardships of his job that much of the clothing that was brought in for examination was not clean. Often it was very dirty, sometimes bloodstained. It made Leguyader's job more than ever distasteful at times. Especially when it showed nothing, as this clothing did.

He badly needed a drink and, feeling martyred, decided to take it out of Sergeant Darcy by ringing him at home. Unfortunately Darcy, possessing the temperament he did, was the last man in the world to be upset by Leguyader and he only irritated him further by the cheerful greeting he offered.

'I've been through that clothing of Chenandier's,' Leguyader announced, gloomily frustrated. 'There's nothing. No blood. No bone. Nothing. Just a couple of hairs belonging to his wife.'

'You could hardly condemn a man for that,' Darcy said. 'They could have got there as he kissed her goodbye.'

'Would he kiss her goodbye? I understood he didn't sleep with her.'

'Well, you never know,' Darcy said pointedly. 'Happiness is as scarce these days as hen's teeth and he might have gone mad.'

Leguyader sniffed. 'It's not enough to suggest he murdered her, though, is it? They'd probably been there for years.'

Darcy sighed. 'Well, that seems to write Chenandier off,' he said.

'Unless he had some other clothes hidden away we don't know about.'

'Which we don't. Thanks. I'll tell the old man when he comes in tomorrow.'

Leguyader was conscious of having been unnecessarily terse and he tried to make amends. 'How's it going?' he asked.

'We could do with a break.'

*   *   *

As it happened, though Darcy didn't know it, a break was on the way, because at that moment in the Place de la Libération in the centre of the city, Madame Marie-Ange de St Juste, who lived in an apartment overlooking the semi-circular parking lot opposite the Palais des Ducs, was in the process of watching a man studying the cars that were just beginning in the increasing heat to build up an inside temperature that would take away their owners' breath when they returned to unlock them. The man wore a cap and a checked shirt and blue cotton trousers, and hardly looked the type to own anything as expensive as the big Citroën he was staring at. Madame de St Juste was an old woman and, because she was confined to her apartment but was still interested in what went on, she had always enjoyed studying the people who moved in and out of the palace opposite her room. Her window was a gazebo type that gave her a view of the square and the Rue Rameau as far as the Eglise St Michel, and her major joy in life was watching everything that went on.

Now, as she watched, the man in the flat cap moved from the Citroën to a Peugeot—from her window, Madame de St Juste had learned to recognise cars as well as she recognised her own family—and was studying it carefully. He stared at the front then at the back, then moved on to a Deux Chevaux alongside. He quite obviously wasn't the owner of any of the cars and he quite obviously was more interested in them than he ought to be.

Her bird-like face against the glass, Madame de St Juste watched him for a little while longer, as he moved round a Ferrari, a British Maxi with a buckled fender and an American Dodge, and then began to study the French cars that were ranged in rows, red, blue, yellow, orange, all building up a temperature in the sun like pressure cookers. He was clearly up to no good and Madame de St Juste knew exactly where her duty lay.

Sitting in her window, unable to do much else but look—at the age of eighty-one there wasn't much else you could do but look—she had often noticed things that other people missed, and on one occasion had even been recommended by the police for her alertness in spotting a man trying to break into the bar facing the palace. She glanced at the bar now and noticed a policeman standing in the doorway talking to the proprietor, for whom she had always had a fondness because on hot days he sent her up cold drinks when she telephoned. She glanced again at the man by the cars. He was still engaged in whatever it was he was doing and it seemed too good an opportunity to miss. The police recommendation had gone to Madame de St Juste's head a little.

When Pel reached his office next day, he was feeling like a new man. With the aid of Didier Darras, he had left home with Madame Routy already showing signs of frayed nerves.

'You must be a detective, too, when you grow up,' she had urged over breakfast in that manner of silly women who hadn't the foggiest idea how to talk to small boys.

'I don't want to be a detective,' Didier had said firmly.

'Good idea,' Pel had agreed. 'Much better to be a plain traffic cop, then you can enjoy sticking parking tickets on examining magistrates' cars when they leave them where they shouldn't.'

As he entered headquarters he was almost smiling. But not for long because Judge Brisard met him in the corridor and followed him into his office, demanding to know how the investigation was proceeding.

'Slowly,' Pel said shortly.

'Too slowly, do you think, Inspector?'

Pel smiled. It looked like the smile on the face of a tiger. 'If you're not happy, Judge,' he pointed out, 'you could launch a police action yourself. A judge can.'

It was enough to make Brisard back off sharply and Pel marched down the corridor to his office, well content. Two small triumphs in a matter of an hour was something to crow about. First Madame Routy and now Brisard. In his efforts to avoid bureaucratic inertia in his area of authority, Brisard behaved sometimes as if someone had attached electric wires to his backside and kept giving him a shock. It

was a pleasure to slow him down. It only needed Nosjean to
have his snotty nose rubbed in the dust and the day was
complete. Pel was actually humming to himself as he
headed for his office.

Nosjean stared after him, startled, as he swept past. 'The
Old Man sounds cheerful for a change,' he said. 'What's
that he's whistling?'

'My grandmother used to sing that as she rolled pastry,'
Darcy said. 'Probably my great-grandmother, too. It's
Froufrou.'

Nosjean looked awed. 'That's centuries old. Why's he
singing *that*?'

Darcy shrugged. 'He's probably never learned anything
new since he was a kid.'

Nosjean stared in front of him, his mind going like the
inside of a pin-ball machine. 'Well, it could be all right,' he
conceded. 'Hotted up and given a bit of decent backing.'

Pel had just taken his place at his desk when Darcy
appeared.

'We're in luck, Patron,' he said. 'The uniformed boys
have just this minute rung to say they've picked up the
gardener.'

'Where was he?'

Darcy grinned and gestured to the window. 'Right there.
In the city. In the Place de la Libération. Some chap who'd
never heard of Chenandier pulled him in on suspicion of
trying to steal a car. And fair enough, after all; he's got a
record for that sort of thing.'

'Where is he now?'

'Where Darcq was: below. Sweating it out. I had a little
preliminary chat with him. Leaned on him, you might say.
He didn't have much to offer so I decided to leave him for
you, Chief. He's tougher than he seems. He's naturalised,
by the way, I've discovered. But only recently, so you might
say he's a bit naïve as far as France is concerned. On the
other hand, he's not such a fool as he pretends, either.'

Pel gestured. 'Let's have him out at Aigunay. I'll talk to
him there. It'll be better. If he knows anything, it'll probably worry him.'

'Right, Chief.' Darcy reached behind the door and, pulling out a suitcase, placed it on Pel's desk and slid a sheet of paper across. 'The clothes Chenandier had in Paris,' he said. 'And Leguyader's report. Negative. Negative. Negative.'

Pel frowned. 'No trace of anything?'

'Nothing at all.' Darcy leaned on the suitcae. 'I've rung the hotel in Paris, by the way. They identified the suits. They say they never saw him in anything else. And Sergeant Lagé telephoned all the restaurants and business acquaintances he mentioned. They all vouch for him.'

He began to open the suitcase and Pel watched him sourly.

'What now?'

Darcy flung the lid back.

'Notice anything, Patron?'

'Well, go on. Don't keep me in suspense. What?'

Darcy lifted up a sweater. It was heavy and ugly and made of wool. 'Pretty warm for the time of the year, don't you think?' he said. 'Even for the north. And somehow not quite Chenandier. His tastes are slicker. He might have been tight with money, but he doesn't seem to have kept himself short. He has monogrammed underwear, I noticed.'

He was lucky, Pel thought. Pel still wore wool next to the skin. When it was winter, his blood needed to be kept going round all those little veins and things, and when the wind blew off the mountains of the Jura or the Vosges and the snow came, it actually seemed to congeal. He was often ashamed of his woollen underwear and prayed that he'd never be run over and killed, so that he'd be undressed at the mortuary by someone who knew him. They'd never stop laughing.

'It doesn't go with him,' Darcy said, indicating the sweater.

'Why do you think that?'

'Something about him. He's no chicken but he's very much with it. I bet the girls like him.'

'Why do you say that?'

'People in the know can tell.'

'And you're in the know?'

Darcy grinned. 'I'm a fornicologist,' he said. 'I go in for it a lot myself. I dare bet a meteorologist can smell another meteorologist a mile off. And a metallurgist a metallurgist. I bet *he's* a fornicologist, too.'

'Go on,' Pel said, impressed in spite of himself.

Darcy responded with enthusiasm. 'As a connoisseur of earnest-minded virgins of good character,' he said, 'I know what they like to see.' He hoisted up the sweater again. 'And this isn't it.'

'What are you getting at?'

'It's not Paris wear. If I'd been going away for a week in Paris, I'd have taken something smarter than this. There's nothing more embarrassing than this sort of thing when a girl's watching you shining-eyed from the pillow as you undress.'

Pel stared broodingly at Darcy, wondering why he hadn't the same knowledge as his sergeant. God, he felt, had designed him specifically as a woman-queller.

'Perhaps he didn't go to Paris for the sort of thing you go for,' he said. 'And perhaps he feels the cold. I do. I have thin blood. It's something in the system. I think I should drink more red wine. They say it's good for the circulation.'

Darcy hadn't finished yet. He produced a folder which he laid in front of Pel. 'Seen these, Patron?' he asked.

Pel looked at the folder as if it might bite. 'What are they?'

'Dirty pictures. I found them in Chenandier's room.'

Pel opened the folder. He'd never had much time for eroticism. He'd seen too many naked women—mostly very dead—to have any feelings about uncovered female flesh.

'Men don't go in for this sort of thing when they're happy with their wives,' Darcy pointed out.

'Perhaps he *wasn't* all that happy,' Pel said. 'Despite the way he behaves. They don't mean a thing.'

'Maybe not,' Darcy said. 'But it isn't quite the picture he was trying to give us of himself yesterday, is it? Think he had something going with Quermel? After all, she looked

after his clothes, and that's a job that could lead to com-
plications.'

Pel nodded thoughtfully. 'Especially,' he agreed, 'if it
entailed calling her into the bedroom for consultations
while his wife was out. Let's go and see the gardener.'

CHAPTER
EIGHT

The gardener, a dark man, tall for one of his race and not
very old, spoke a curious French that was hard to understand. He was sitting on the sack-covered chair by the
littered bench in the little shed where he took his meals
behind Chenandier's house. A uniformed policeman
leaned on the whitewashed wall where he'd written his
pencilled reminders.

As Pel appeared the Italian rose, but the Inspector
waved to him to sit down again.

'You Giacomo Albertini?' he asked.

'Si, Signore.'

'Naturalised, I understand.'

'Si, Signore. I married a French girl and took out papers.'
The Italian shrugged. 'But she die two years ago and I sell
the house and move in with a family in Bazay.'

'You were trying to steal a car.'

The Italian looked worried. 'No, Signore. I cannot.'

'Why not?'

'I cannot drive.'

Pel frowned. 'You've got a motobicyclette.'

'I haven't a licence to drive a car.'

'Doesn't mean you can't drive one.'

'No, Signore. I promise you.'

The Italian twisted his hands but it didn't pluck at any of
Pel's heart-strings. He'd seen it too often. 'You were going
to steal something from one then,' he said. 'You were
looking for one that was unlocked.'

'Why should I, Signore?'

'Because you've got a record for that sort of thing.'

The Italian shrugged. 'No, Signore,' he said. 'It is not that.'

'Then what *were* you doing?'

'I just like cars.'

'What sort of cars?'

'All sorts.'

Pel's eyes flickered. 'What sort of car has Monsieur Chenandier got?' he asked.

'A Merc.' The Italian answered immediately. 'A Mercedes like Signor Laye.'

'You like cars enough to steal them?'

'I tell you, Signore, I cannot even drive.'

'My car's out there,' Pel said. 'Can you see it?'

'Just, Signore.'

'What sort is it?'

'I don't know.'

'You like cars, but you can't recognise mine?'

The Italian's expression was cool. 'It doesn't look a very exciting car, Signore,' he said.

Pel frowned. The Italian was right. It was the sort of car a hard-working, underpaid, chronically sick police inspector might own, while crooks, thieves and layabouts owned big Citroëns, Peugeots and Mercs.

'What were you doing if you weren't going to steal anything?' he said.

'Looking at the cars, Signore. That's all.'

'Which part of the cars?'

'The number plates.'

'Why?'

'I'm interested in them. I always have been. I have never a car of my own so I look at other people's—how they're made, how fast they go, where they come from.'

'I'm still surprised you haven't a car of your own. People as keen on them as you seem to be usually manage to acquire one somehow. Why did you disappear?'

'I thought they'd think it was me.'

Pel glanced at Darcy. 'Think *what* was you?'

'Madame. I had nothing to do with it. I didn't kill her.'

'How did you know she was dead?'

'The papers say so, Signore.'

'Not until the morning afterwards. You disappeared the night before. You weren't in your lodgings for breakfast. Your landlady told the police so.'

The Italian looked worried. 'Then perhaps I hear someone say so.'

'Who?'

'I do not remember, Signore.'

'Sure you weren't responsible for it yourself?'

The Italian's eyes widened. 'Oh, no, Signore! Madonna, no!'

Darcy leaned on the little bench beneath all the scrawled pencil messages. 'You have a record,' he pointed out. 'There was an assault case.'

'That was a long time ago, Signore.'

'Four years. That's not long.'

'I am provoked, Signore. They call me a dirty Italian.'

'Who did?'

'These men.'

Pel glanced at Darcy who nodded. 'That's what the file says, Patron. A bar in Dijon.'

'And the attempt at blackmail?'

The Italian frowned. 'A man I work for. He does not pay me enough and when I see him with a girl, I try to get more money out of him. I say I will tell his wife.'

'And?'

'He beats me up. Then he report me to the police.'

Darcy grinned. 'Well, if you will pick somebody tougher than yourself.'

Pel tried another approach. 'You knew Madame Chenandier was dead, didn't you? The night she died.'

The Italian's eyes fell. 'No, Signore.'

'Then why did you hide?'

'I am working late at my allotment and bring my fork back. I have a few drinks at a bar—'

'What time was this?'

'10.30. About that. There is a man in the lane and I hear shouting, so I do not go near the place.'

'Where did you go? You didn't go home?'

'I stay with my sister. She marries a man from Boux.'

'Why did you go there?'

The Italian shrugged. 'It is raining and Boux is nearer than Bazay, also I want someone to talk to. Someone who speaks my language. I do not have many friends. When I arrive here next morning I see the police and know something has happened, so I leave again. I know it is bad because there are cars and a lot of uniforms.'

'The night before when you heard the shouting: Did you investigate? Go a bit closer? Have a look?'

'No, Signore.' The Italian's eyes rolled. 'I go to Boux.'

Pel knew Boux. He had an aunt there whom he'd been obliged for years to visit on Sunday. He'd spent many hours bored in Boux. It lay on high ground with, behind, a confused mass of valleys formed by the slopes of rounded hills that fell away to the river. The only time he liked Boux was in October when the heat gave body to the odour of new wine that floated over the whole countryside. The wine was the only part of Boux that Pel had ever enjoyed.

'That's a long way,' he said.

'Si, Signore.'

'It was late. There'd be no buses. How did you get there? Car?'

'The motobicyclette. It gets me to and from work. I get it second-hand. It's red.'

'And the next morning when you saw the police? What did you think?'

'I think Monsieur kills her.'

'Why did you think that?'

'Because she has men. He must have known. He is not a fool, Signore.' The Italian gestured with his right hand and left forearm. 'Once he asked me if I ever see visitors in the house when he is away.'

'What did you say?'

'It isn't my business.'

'When you brought your fork back here the night of the

murder—did you see Madame Chenandier with a man that night?'

'No, Signore. But there is a car in the lane that evening. Drawn up in the shadows under the trees.'

'Whose car?'

'Monsieur Laye's. From next door.'

'Was he the man you saw in the lane?'

The Italian gestured. 'Well, it is dark and he is in the shadows. But as I pass him I see him against the lights of the house. I think he might be a footpad and get my fork ready. Then I decide it is Monsieur Chenandier.'

'Why?'

'Same shape, Signore. Same build. It looks like him.'

'Did he say anything?'

'I think he tries *not* to be seen.'

Pel paused. 'What do you know of the murdered woman?' he asked.

'Nothing, Signore. She just pay me my wages.'

'Not Monsieur Chenandier?'

'He is never here when I am.'

'Was anybody?'

The Italian's face twisted. '*Non lo capisco*, Signore. I don't understand.'

'I think you do,' Pel said.

The gardener's eyes became wily. 'Once I see a man,' he said. 'Twice. But—' he shrugged '—it may perhaps have been the doctor on a visit. It may have been anybody. *Non lo so*. I do not know. It is not my business. I do not look. I spend my time in the garden and eat my food at midday here in the shed. Sometimes the housekeeper gives me a cup of coffee. She treat me like a human being.'

'Didn't Madame Chenandier?'

'No, Signore. And the daughter, she—'

The Italian paused and Pel saw a shifty look in his eyes. 'What did the daughter do?' he asked.

The Italian fidgeted then he gave an angry gesture. 'She try once to get me in the shed one day when everybody is out.'

'Why?'

Albertini shrugged. 'I think she just want to be near me.'

'Why should you think that?'

'We have talked sometimes. She seem lonely, so I smile a bit. To make her feel better. She is a girl and she is young. That is all. But this day she push up to me. I am doing something on the bench and I keep feeling her against me. Then she offer me money.'

'What for?'

'What *would* she be offering me money for, Signore?'

'Well, tell me. What?'

'She want me to make love to her. Here. In the shed.'

'What did you do?'

'I push her out. So she burst into tears and threatened to tell her father I try to rape her.'

'Because you'd refused to have anything to do with her?'

'Yes.'

'And did she?'

'Madame Quermel tell me later that she did. He laughs at her.'

Pel thought of the lonely, unloved girl looking for affection and in her clumsy thick-headed way even making a mess of that.

'Did she never have any boyfriends?'

'I never see any.'

'But you knew Madame did?'

'It wasn't my business, Signore.'

'What did you *think*?'

'Signore?'

'What did you *think*? Did you think this man you saw *was* the doctor?'

'No, Signore.'

'Why not?'

'He and Madame are too close to each other. They are holding each other.'

'How?'

'How do men and women hold each other, Signore?'

'Well, how do they?'

'Monsieur Chenandier—'

'What about Monsieur Chenandier?'

'Well, he and Madame Quermel—'

'What about them?'

'They hold each other.'

'You saw them?'

'Si, Signore. One morning early. I think Madame Chenandier has been drinking the night before because she does not appear until later in the day, and they are in the kitchen. Madame Quermel is wearing a housecoat and he has just come in from taking exercise and is in a blue track-suit. He has been jog-trotting.'

Darcy smiled. 'You can see 'em every morning before eight, he said. 'On Sunday they come out in hordes. They run down the Cours de Gaulle from the Place Wilson, round the Parc de la Colombière and along the bank of the Ouche. If they've got any energy and breath left, they then run back. Usually they walk.'

Pel listened with interest. He never took any exercise himself beyond a strenuous game of boules.

'And this man who was holding Madame Chenandier,' he went on to the gardener. 'Big man? Small? Fat? Thin?'

'Tall, Signore. Well-built.'

'Monsieur Chenandier's tall and well-built. Couldn't it have been him?'

The Italian frowned. 'I do not think Monsieur ever holds her like that.'

'Why not?'

The Italian shrugged. 'I think perhaps they do not get on well.'

'Why do you think that?'

'Italians know such things.

'Well, that's one way, I suppose,' Darcy observed.

Pel gestured and the Italian continued. 'Also he never talks to her as he talk to Madame Quermel,' he said.

Pel leaned forward. 'How *did* he talk to Madame Quermel?'

'Very quietly, Signore. In corners. When he thinks I am not looking.'

Pel was silent for a while and the Italian rose slowly.

'May I go now, Signore? He indicated the garden. 'I

suppose I must carry on working. I have not been told to leave.'

'What do you do?'

The Italian gestured at the garden. 'Everything. I dig, plant, trim, weed. The hedges, the lawns, the drive, small repairs.'

'What sort of repairs?'

'To the lawn-mower. Occasionally I put screws back in door handles if they fall out. That sort of thing. I also clean the cars.'

Pel indicated the scrawled notes and telephone numbers on the whitewashed wall. 'That your diary?'

The Italian managed a twisted smile. 'I do not read and write well, Signore. I do not know France well. I use it to remind me. I think they are badly spelt. I also put down telephone numbers I am likely to need. Then if I want seed delivering, or fertiliser, if I need a mechanic to do something I cannot do, or if I want tools sharpening, I use the kitchen telephone.'

Pel nodded and gestured and, as the Italian moved off in his slow gardener's trudge to the kitchen, he lit a cigarette. It was in the nature of a celebration, because he had a feeling that things had started to move at last, and it made it worth risking cancer. He saw Darcy smiling at him, and his good humour vanished at once.

'What are you grinning at?'

'You, Patron. I know you. Things are beginning to click a bit, aren't they?'

Pel nodded grudgingly and Darcy went on. 'This chap he saw,' he said. 'Could it have been Chenandier?'

'Chenandier was in Paris. Perhaps it was someone who *looked* like Chenandier. Laye, for instance. Perhaps Laye was this man other people have seen and never identified.'

'Where's Chenandier now?'

'Out.'

'Right,' Pel said. 'I think we'll go and have a chat with that housekeeper then.'

'Estelle? Right, Patron. I'll find her.'

Pel looked up coldly. 'What did you call her?'

'Estelle, Patron. Estelle Quermel. I always believe in getting to first name terms.'

'Especially with women.'

'They talk better that way, Chief.'

'They're also easier pushovers.'

When Madame Quermel appeared in Chenandier's study, she was wearing a summery dress and had done her hair high on her head because of the heat. She looked a good deal younger than her thirty-six years. Pel gestured at a chair and she sat down, her face grave, her manner nervous.

'The night of the murder,' Pel said. 'Was there a car in the lane?'

'I don't know.' She frowned, trying to concentrate. 'There might have been, but I can't tell. My rooms overlook the garden.' She moved her shoulders uncertainly. 'But I wouldn't have seen anything even on that side. I'm in the roof and I look out on the chimney pots and beyond them across the fields. I can't see the garden itself.'

'What about when you returned from your outing?'

'I didn't see anything. No, wait a minute! Monsieur Laye's car was in the lane.'

Pel nodded. 'How did you and Madame Chenandier get on?' he asked.

She gestured with her hand, see-sawing it from side to side. 'So-so.'

'What does that mean?'

'We got on.'

'Did you like her?'

'No.'

'Did she like you?'

'I don't think so.'

Pel paused, thinking. 'I understand you were the one who checked Monsieur Chenandier's clothes,' he went on.

She looked defiant. 'Somebody had to. She never did.'

Pel's eyebrows rose but he said nothing and she hurried on as if it seemed to need an explanation. 'Monsieur Chenandier's a meticulous person.'

'In what way?'

'Careful with money. Everything has to be just so.'

'Are you in love with Monsieur Chenandier?'

She shook her head, but she kept her eyes down. 'No,' she said. 'I felt sorry for him, that's all.'

'What do you know of Monsieur and Madame Chenandier?' Pel asked.

'How do you mean?'

'Did they get on?'

'He hated her.'

She spoke sharply, vituperatively, and Pel sat quietly for a moment.

'How do you know?' he asked eventually. 'Did he tell you?'

Madame Quermel's composure slipped. 'Yes—that is— well, yes, he did.'

'Why should he tell *you*?'

'Perhaps he felt he had to tell *someone*. There wasn't much between him and his daughter.'

'Didn't he have any women friends he might have told?'

She blushed. 'I think there were some.'

'You, for instance?'

She didn't meet Pel's eyes.

'Were you lovers?'

'No.'

'Monsieur Chenandier seems to have a reputation with women.'

'Has he?'

'Didn't you know?'

'No.'

'Everybody else does. Did he never make advances to you?'

'No.'

'Then why was he seen holding you—whispering to you?'

'He didn't.'

'There's a witness. Did he ever come to your room?'

She hesitated, intimidated by his manner. 'Once. He came home early and his wife was out. He came to ask where she was.'

'Did he stay?'

She paused, her eyes downcast. 'Yes.'

'How long?'

'Two hours or so.'

'What did you do? Just talk?'

'No.'

'What?'

'Do I have to say?'

'Not really. I can guess. How many times did he come? Regularly?'

She struggled to speak. 'Not at first. Later, yes.'

'Did he ask you to marry him?'

'He was married already.'

'I've noticed that married men usually manage to get over that little problem. They start by offering to get a divorce. Did he?'

She still refused to meet Pel's eyes. 'He did mention it. He said he'd like to get a divorce but that she wouldn't give him one.' She looked up angrily. 'He'd have seen her all right for money. And she had plenty of men friends.'

'Oh? Who were they?'

'I don't know. She was careful. But I heard their voices sometimes and found cigarettes. That sort of thing.'

Pel sat still for a moment. 'He won't need a divorce now,' he said gently. 'Will you marry him when things have quietened down?'

She looked at him miserably. 'He hasn't asked me.'

'Do you still feel the same about him?'

'Yes.'

'And does he feel the same about you?'

'Yes.'

Pel nodded and changed the direction of his questioning abruptly. 'The night of the murder: When you say you were attacked on your way to see your relatives at St Antoine. You didn't go to St Antoine, did you?'

She stared back at him, her eyes hot. 'Yes.'

'You were *never* in the habit of visiting your relatives at St Antoine. They've told us so. Where were you, in fact?'

She paused unhappily. 'In the city.'

'Where?'

'Down the Cours de Gaulle.'

'What were you doing there?'

'Thinking. I was worried.'

'What about?'

She gave him an anguished look. 'Monsieur Chenandier. The way he and his wife behaved. I thought I was becoming involved and I didn't want to be.'

The heat seemed to be increasing, and the house in the Chemin de Champs-Loups felt stuffy. There was no breeze and, with the shutters closed against the sun, it had the atmosphere of a funeral parlour. Though the salon was sealed off now, it was hard to forget what had happened in there and, though they could hear Madame Quermel moving about in the kitchen, she was quiet, as if she were brooding on what she'd been forced to disclose.

'I think we need a drink,' Pel said. 'Let's go along to the bar.'

'Well, we're not likely to get a coffee from Quermel this morning,' Darcy smiled. 'That's for sure.'

They elected to sit outside the restaurant on the plastic chairs. Ordering beers, Darcy put up the sunshade advertising Martini, and they sat silently, smoking and drinking, Darcy's eyes on the girl who served them. She was busy behind the zinc counter inside now, daubing another layer of black make-up on her lashes. There was so much on them by this time, she was having to blink to separate them, and she'd been to the hairdresser since they'd last seen her so that her hair was frizzed until it looked as if it had been fried.

'Women always think they can get away with it,' Pel said suddenly.

Darcy's eyes were still on the girl. 'They get too embroiled in gadgetry,' he agreed. 'All that stuff they put on only gets in a man's way when he goes into a clinch. Yet, take it away, and he wouldn't even look at half of them.'

Pel turned and stared at the girl. 'I was thinking of Quermel,' he said coldly.

'Oh!' Darcy grinned. 'Think she was lying, Chief?'

'Yes. But how much I don't know.'

'That's a funny story the gardener told about Odile: Trying to get him to make love to her.'

Pel nodded, brooding. The atmosphere in the Chenandier house had worried him, but he felt better now. For a sick and ailing old man, in fact, he felt not too bad. Not fit, of course, but better.

'If I'd been the gardener,' Darcy said, 'it wouldn't have been Odile I'd have had my eye on. It would have been Quermel. She's got something, that one.'

Pel lit a cigarette, wondering, as he broke his vow yet again, why God didn't strike him down with a flash of lightning. 'You should keep your eye on the ball,' he said.

'Nothing wrong with having a pretty woman around, Chief. There are always plenty in the 007 books.'

'You should stick to Maigret,' Pel advised. 'Less sex. Let's go and talk to the girl.'

When Odile Chenandier appeared, Pel pretended for a while not to notice her. Eventually he looked up and she gave him her worried stare.

'Madame Quermel tells me your father was a meticulous person,' Pel said. 'Always exact. Careful with money. Always very precise. In everything he did. Would *you* say that of your father?'

The girl studied him warily. She was dressed now in a vest bearing the words, 'Chicago Red Sox', across her breasts and a pair of faded frayed jeans that fitted skin-tight to her behind. She obviously tried hard to make herself attractive to the opposite sex and Pel had seen her more than once eyeing Darcy. But there was a lost sort of naïvity about her that ruined her efforts, and curiously, it made him think of Nosjean. He repeated the question.

'He was clever.'

There was something in the way she spoke that made Pel lean forward. 'Clever? How?'

'In running his life. He always seemed in control of it.'

'Something you envied.'

'Yes. I never seem—' she stopped and gestured help-lessly.

'How did you get on with him?'

She sighed. 'I loved him. I loved my mother. I wanted them to love me. But it didn't seem to work out. My mother was always too busy and my father was—' her hand flapped again in its curiously limp, hopeless movement—'he was too busy, too.'

She seemed so lost Pel hesitated before he flung his next question at her. 'Did you know we found traces of blood on one of your shoes?' he said.

She looked startled. 'Well, it was all over the place,' she said with a shudder. 'Up the walls. On the ceiling. On the door.'

'You said you didn't go into the room where your mother was found.'

'No, I didn't.'

'Then how did you get blood on your shoe?'

Her eyes filled with tears and she gave him a frightened look.

'You did go in, didn't you?'

'Yes.'

'Why did you go in? Why didn't you just telephone the police at once from the kitchen? It must have been obvious she wasn't alive.'

She hesitated then gave him an anguished look. 'I wanted to see her,' she said. 'She'd always gone on so about being beautiful and how well she could sing. I wanted to see what she looked like now that she wasn't beautiful and couldn't sing any more.'

Pel eyed her curiously. 'That's an unusual attitude, isn't it?' he said.

She gave him a swift look, full of the high, hurt rage of youth that for a second almost transformed her plain features.

'It wasn't for me,' she said.

Pel studied her for a while. Her sallow skin was pink with anger and indignation.

'Why do you say that?'

'She never helped me much.'

'Did anyone?'

She didn't meet his eyes but kept her gaze on the floor as she shook her head.

'Had you no friends?'

Her head shook again.

'What about the gardener?'

She lifted her head abruptly and the frightened look came back. 'What has he said?'

'He told us about you. How you made advances to him in his shed.'

Her face crumpled. 'He's lying. It was him who made eyes at me. He wasn't all that old and he—' she shook her head and flapped her hands again in a lost, tragic little gesture '—well, he was quite nice-looking. I used to like to be with him. Even when I was much younger. But there was never anything like that.'

'He says you offered him money.'

'No. Well—yes, I did. Once. His shirt was torn. You could see his skin through it. It was very brown. He looked strong. He said he couldn't afford another, and I offered to buy one for him.'

'He said you offered the money because you wanted him to make love to you. He said you threatened him if he didn't.'

Her mouth had opened and her eyes had widened. She looked shocked. 'No,' she said. 'No! I never asked him to make love to me!' Her voice lowered as if she were ashamed. 'I didn't know how. I wanted so much for my mother to tell me how to attract men, but she never did. I thought she was the most beautiful thing I'd ever seen and all I wanted was to be like her. But I don't think she ever really cared about me. She just regarded me as a nuisance. Because I wasn't beautiful and I wasn't clever. And she wanted all the limelight for herself.' Now that she had started talking, she seemed unable to stop. 'The only time a man ever came to see me—he was my cousin from Arles— she got him in the library and spent the whole afternoon talking and laughing with him, and in the end I went outside and left them to it.' She raised her eyes to Pel and behind her wide, pale eyes, he felt he was looking into her soul. It looked desperately lonely, and for a moment her misery seemed to lift her features out of their drab nonentity.

'I never asked him to make love to me,' she said. 'He was the gardener and I was the daughter of the house.' She paused and her voice dropped to a whisper. 'Though sometimes I wished he would.' She gazed at Pel in agony. 'Nobody's ever made love to me, Inspector. Nobody's ever wanted to.'

CHAPTER
NINE

Because of the heat and the distance from the city, Pel didn't fancy the long drive back and they decided to risk their digestion once more at the bar-restaurant in the village.

The place was full of men in blue overalls and caps, all leaning on the counter over their drinks. A woman with two children and a man who, judging by the pamphlets spread on the table around him, was a commercial traveller for drinks, were eating at the plain, square, paper-covered tables. The girl behind the counter was still at it with the eye make-up and Darcy stared at her in amazement.

'If she puts any more on,' he said, 'she'll be top heavy.'

At least there were tripes, but they'd been cooked without flair and, inevitably, Pel wished he'd chosen the chicken. By this time, the girl had noticed Darcy's eyes on her and, after she'd served them, persisted in standing by their table talking. It irritated Pel because he wanted to think.

'She seems to suffer from a cabalistic fantasy that she's got a fatal fascination for men,' he observed when she finally disappeared.

'She looks better when she smiles,' Darcy said. 'Women always do.'

Pel grunted, thinking about Odile Chenandier. Just for a moment, he felt, it had been her unhappiness that had made her sallow features almost attractive.

Chenandier himself had returned from the city when they got back to the house. He was wearing a lightweight checked suit and a pale blue shirt. Though he had no pretensions to good looks, he looked as virile as a bull and it was obvious what it was about him that attracted women.

'Well, Inspector,' he asked. 'Arrested that brother-in-law of mine yet?'

'Not yet,' Pel said.

'He'll disappear.'

'He'd better not.'

Pel gestured at a chair and Chenandier sat down. 'Ironic, isn't it?' he observed ruefully. 'That you invite me to sit down in my own house.'

'You can always stand,' Darcy growled.

Pel pulled his notebook forward. 'This trip to Paris,' he began.

Chenandier smiled. 'Back on that, are we? I was there. You can ask all my customers.'

Pel didn't mention that they already had. Somehow he didn't like Chenandier. He was a smooth-looking man, and bringeurs—smoothies—were always anathema to Pel, who considered he himself had a face like the Phantom of the Opera, no style with his clothes, a social manner that would have disgraced a half-wit, and an acute shortage of money which always served to highlight all his other defects.

'I thought I'd ask again,' he said.

Chenandier shrugged. 'You'll get the same answer, Inspector,' he pointed out. 'I'm no parlour hero. That takes some talent for lying and a great deal of skill in remembering your own lines. It's easier to tell the truth, I've found.'

Pel studied his finger nails for a while then, saddened at his own miserable lack of will, lit another cigarette. Any minute now, he thought, he'd drop dead with cancer of the lung. The way he smoked, in fact, it was a wonder everybody who came into contact with him didn't drop dead of it, too.

'This running you did,' he said. 'Was it because you were concerned for your health?' He spoke as if he could appreciate how Chenandier might feel about such a delicate subject.

Chenandier smiled. 'Not particularly. I just liked to keep fit.'

'You're a strong man?'

'I suppose so.'

'And, being an ex-para, pretty tough, too, I imagine?'

'Yes, I suppose so.'

'Not given to cosseting yourself?'

'I never have.'

Pel looked up and blinked. 'Then why do you wear such heavy sweaters, Monsieur?'

Chenandier stared, frowning. 'I don't.'

'You did when you went to Paris. Or at least, you took one with you. Why would that be?'

Chenandier smiled. 'That's Madame Quermel. She looks after me a bit. She packs for me. She thinks I'm a little boy. And Paris is north.'

'Not that far north.' Pel studied him with his dark sad eyes. 'Yours was a *very* warm sweater.'

'I suppose it was. But I don't make a habit of wearing it. I don't like that kind of sweater. But because I don't make a habit of wearing it doesn't mean I don't possess it. It's what you might call an insurance. I get recurrences of malaria. But I don't believe in letting it stop me doing what I have to do. I simply go slower, put on warmer clothes and dose myself well. You'll remember I told you: I served in Indo-China.'

'That was something you could be proud of,' Pel said.

'I was. I still am. It wasn't our fault that we failed. It was the high-ups.'

'It usually is when things go wrong,' Pel said, thinking of Judge Brisard and the Procureur.

He glanced at Darcy. It was an arrangement they often had. When Pel gave Darcy his special look, it was for Darcy to take over the questioning to allow him to get his own thoughts in order.

Darcy jumped in with both feet. He enjoyed questioning and considered himself good at it. He wasn't, of course. No one, Pel felt, was any good—except Evariste Clovis Désiré Pel. Darcy lacked subtlety, though he complemented Pel perfectly by doing all the horsework so that Pel could do the thinking, and now he went at it like Margueritte's cavalry at Sedan. He slapped the dirty pictures they'd found on the table in front of Chenandier. 'Know anything about these?' he asked.

Chenandier studied the pictures without changing his expression. 'Oh, you found those, did you? They don't make me a man with homicidal tendencies.'

'Whose are they?'

'Mine.'

'Where did you get them?'

'They were given to me in Paris. Some time ago.'

'Who by?'

'A customer. Revolting man. But, like relatives, you don't choose the people you do business with.'

'Mean anything to you?'

'The pictures? Not much.'

Darcy seemed to be getting nowhere and Pel wondered what he was aiming at. Trying to prove to Chenandier he was frustrated enough to find a mistress, he assumed.

'What was the relationship between you and your wife, Monsieur?' Darcy asked.

Chenandier shrugged. 'The same as most people when they've been married twenty-five years. We got on but the gilt had rubbed off the gingerbread a bit, I suppose.'

'What does that mean? Did you love her?'

'Yes. At least as much as she loved me.'

'Can you enlarge on that?'

Chenandier looked at Darcy. 'How old are you, mon brave?' he asked and Darcy answered without thinking.

'Twenty-nine.'

'By the time you're forty-nine you'll realise that marriage isn't sitting cosily holding hands in front of the television or reading a book while your wife knits. All with odd moments of high sexual ecstasy.'

Pel saw that Darcy had lost the initiative and needed rescuing before he got another flea in his ear. 'Did you still make love to your wife, Monsieur?' he asked, joining in briskly.

'Occasionally.'

'Even though you hated her?'

'I didn't hate her.'

'I've heard you did.'

Chenandier lost his composure for the first time. 'Who told you that? Odile?'

'Never mind who. *Did* you hate her?'

'No.'

'But there was something that—shall we say, displeased you?'

Chenandier thought for a long time before answering. 'Well, I suppose you'll have to know eventually, Inspector,' he said. 'She had men friends.'

'You knew?'

'I found out.'

'How?'

'The usual way. I noticed a difference in her manner to me. I was suspicious. Comme mari, je ne suis pas aveugle. As a husband I'm not blind. She stopped being interested in me and I became suspicious. Then I found letters. Once I came home unexpectedly and found her there with a man.'

'Did you know him?'

'No. I gather he was someone she'd met in Paris. He worked for a car hire firm and she'd hired a car from him or something. She did occasionally. She used to get them to run her home when she'd been drinking. Then she used to bring them in and they stayed. They always seemed to be car hire people. They're like car salesmen—a pretty flashy lot, I suppose. Always young and a bit slick. She had them here and in Paris and sometimes when she went to the South.'

'Do you know any names?'

'No.' Chenandier shook his head, reasonable and understanding. 'But eventually they became—well—' he stopped and raised a twisted face '—I often thought she'd find herself in trouble.'

'And you, Monsieur?'

'Me?'

'How did you feel about her?'

Chenandier shrugged. 'I tried to go on loving her. I tried to understand, because I'm away a lot and I knew it must have been lonely. But it worried me, of course.'

'Naturally. But you didn't hate her?'

'Not *hate*.'

'What then?'

Chenandier's shoulders sagged. 'She became like a weight round my shoulders, Inspector. That damned opera. The fact that she once sang in Paris. I grew sick of hearing about it. She was so unintelligent, Inspector. And that silly child she presented me with.'

'What's wrong with her?'

'She's so pathetic, Inspector, she seems to have no life in her.'

It was a classic case of a man successful in business and in his personal life expecting his children to be exactly the same. 'Perhaps she needs encouraging,' Pel said.

Chenandier shrugged and Pel sniffed. 'In any case,' he went on, 'lots of people suffer from those things and manage to live with them.'

'It was the men, I suppose, chiefly.' Chenandier gestured with his hand in a weary sort of way. 'I knew she had them in as soon as I went to Paris.'

'Was it because you were having women in Paris? Which came first?'

'I haven't said I had women in Paris.'

'But you did, didn't you?'

Chenandier nodded. 'Yes.'

Pel leaned forward. 'The night in Paris, the one you can't account for, the next to the last night. The night your wife was murdered. Were you with a woman?'

Chenandier nodded. 'Yes.'

'I thought you went to the Bobino.'

Chenandier was unperturbed. 'I did both.'

Pel frowned. 'Who was this woman you were with? Your mistress?'

'No.'

'You have a mistress?'

'I have had. Not any more. It's over.

'Who was it then—this woman you went with?'

'I don't know.'

'Why not?'

'I've told you. I had too much to drink. I was thinking about my wife. Life was becoming intolerable. I walked. Doing a lot of thinking. And a lot of drinking, too, I suppose. I met this girl and went home with her.'

'And you don't know her name?'

'No idea.'

'Or where she lived?'

'No.' Chenandier looked up. 'Look, Inspector, I can see the way you're thinking. But it wasn't me. I didn't do her in. It could as well have been her brother. He was just the sort. Or—' Chenandier stopped dead then went on in a wondering voice '—or Odile,' he said.

Pel leaned forward. 'Why Odile?"

Chenandier gestured. 'Nothing.'

'Why should Odile want to murder her mother?'

'She didn't like her.'

'Are you sure?'

'Yes, I'm afraid so.'

'Enough to commit murder?' Pel said. 'This kind of brutal murder?'

Chenandier shrugged. 'Perhaps I shouldn't have said that. It was just silliness, really. Poor Odile. We didn't get on. She had a quick temper like my wife. But it was just something that crossed my mind—something I remembered—something—it was nothing.'

Pel wrenched the investigation back to where they'd left it.

'Did you always go with a woman when you went to Paris?'

Chenandier shrugged. 'No. It depended on how bad things had been. If they were bad, I picked someone up.

They didn't argue with me as my wife did. They were even sometimes kind.'

'Were there other women? Here, in this area of France, for instance?'

'No. Only when I went away. I don't believe in fouling my own nest.'

'What about Madame Quermel?'

Chenandier shrugged. 'Her? Not likely.'

'She's not bad-looking. You must have noticed her.'

'I'd noticed her. But it was too close to home.'

'So you never tried anything with her?'

'No. Never.'

'She says you did.'

Chenandier's calm vanished. 'Then she's a liar,' he snapped.

'She's pretty sure.'

Chenandier sagged again. 'Well, once. When I came home late. I was tired and miserable. I went up to her room to ask where my wife was. She made me some chocolate and we sat and talked. She was sympathetic. Perhaps she made something of it. Widows do, you know. They have vivid imaginations.'

Madame Routy hadn't, Pel thought. The only thing that appeared to cross Madame Routy's mind was the way to switch on the television. He cleared his throat noisily and came back to the present.

'You stayed up there, didn't you?' he said.

'No.'

'She says you did. Not once. Many times.'

Chenandier's eyes narrowed. 'I think all women are damned fools,' he said. He nodded. 'Yes, I did. But she meant nothing to me. She was just a bit of fluff.'

'She thought she was more than that.'

'No. You know how women are.'

Pel didn't. 'Tell me,' he said.

'They get things in their minds.'

'Such as believing you said you'd like to get a divorce, but that your wife wouldn't give you one?'

'Did she tell you that?'

'She did.'

'Well, I can only imagine that she's got a very fertile imagination.'

'Or a very good memory,' Pel said. 'She was the woman you mentioned? The woman who was your mistress?'

'Yes. But it's over now. These things do finish, don't they?'

'Have you told her?'

'Yes.'

'Then why does *she* think it isn't over?'

'Women get some funny ideas in their heads. They can't accept that an affair's over unless they see you in bed with another woman.'

Darcy returned to the attack. 'Your wife's jewellery, Monsieur? Have you any idea what there was? Can you give us a complete list?'

Chenandier shrugged. 'Of sorts.' He went to the desk and, rummaging round in the drawer, produced a typed sheet of paper. 'That's a list she made out for insurance. I wouldn't know if it's complete. She was always adding to it, selling off odd pieces and buying others with the money. Odile might know.'

Odile did.

As they talked, the telephone went and Pel snatched it up. 'Pel,' he said.

'Leguyader!' The telephone sounded angry. 'I've got that report on those clothes you sent up—Gervase Darcq's.'

'Go on.'

'Well, first of all, whose bright idea was it to send him in at the end of the day and then tell me to do a check when I couldn't send him home? I was here all night, with him fast asleep in a blanket in the sergeants' room. Whose idea was that?'

'Mine,' Pel said.

'Oh!' Obviously Leguyader hadn't expected that reply. He'd clearly suspected it might have been Nosjean's and had been hoping to be able to tear a strip off him. 'Do you know I went without my dinner?'

'So did I,' Pel said. It wasn't true, but he enjoyed goading Leguyader.

'Oh!' Leguyader said again. He seemed to resent Pel being able to match all his complaints. 'Why?'

'My housekeeper was watching television.'

'Well, mine wasn't,' Leguyader retorted. 'It wasn't due to that at all. It was because I was working. And I couldn't leave because we couldn't turn that big lump, Darcq, out on the streets in his birthday suit. He hadn't any other clothes.'

'I know,' Pel said calmly. 'What did you find?'

'Nothing.' Leguyader seemed delighted that this time it was his turn to score a point.

'Nothing?'

'Nothing at all. Just a lot of food stains. Who is this chap? Does he eat his food by throwing it at his mouth from arm's length?'

'He gets drunk a lot,' Pel said patiently. 'Perhaps that accounts for it.'

'Well, there's nothing.'

'No blood?'

'Not a drop. Just old beer and wine stains. A few unidentified women's hairs, blonde, brunette and red.'

'Doesn't mean a thing. He isn't the type to brush his clothes much. Any of them his sister's?'

'Not one. And you might be interested to hear, too, that we completed the check on the cars. There was no blood there either.'

'On none of 'em?'

'None.' Leguyader sounded delighted at the disappointment in Pel's voice.

Pel replaced the telephone quietly and stood for a while, staring at the instrument, deep in thought. He started to life abruptly.

'Fetch Odile back.'

She returned unwillingly, with her usual mixture of caution and aggressiveness, and Pel decided that, because of her parents, she knew only how to be hostile or wary and was totally at a loss in any situation that demanded anything else.

'Yes,' she said. 'There was a ruby ring. A big one, worth a lot of money. And a treble row of pearls. She also had a sapphire necklace and an amethyst set—ear-rings, necklace, brooch, ring. There was a sapphire-and-diamond ring. An emerald brooch. A zirkon.'

'That the lot?'

'No. There were others.'

'Could you list them from memory?'

'Yes, if necessary.'

'You seem to know them well.'

She frowned and the old agony appeared in her eyes again. 'Of course I do. I was always looking at them, wishing I had some like them. She always said my skin wasn't right for jewels, though. She said you had to have a flawless skin.'

'Did *she*?'

'Yes.'

'Are you sure you liked your mother?'

'I loved her. I thought the world of her. I told you. But she didn't like *me*.'

'How about your father?'

'He just laughed at me. And I think he was busy making eyes at Estelle Quermel.'

'Indeed?'

'Well—' she moved her shoulders in a wildly indifferent shrug that showed her misery '—she liked men, didn't she?'

'Did she?'

'She even made eyes at the gardener.'

Pel decided that she was a prey to agonising jealousies, and tried to be gentle with her. 'Why do you say that?' he asked.

'She used to invite him into the kitchen, didn't she? He was often in there. He was in there only this morning.'

'He went for a coffee. He told me he was going.'

'Then why did they have their heads together?'

'*Did* they have their heads together?'

'Yes. They were whispering.'

'About what?'

She looked puzzled, then baffled. 'They were talking about motor car numbers,' she said.

'He seems to have a fixation about car numbers,' Darcy said.

'Well, I heard her say that 39 was the Jura, and then he asked her what was Paris and she said it was 75.'

'Not very erotic stuff,' Darcy observed.

She flashed him a desperate, hurt glance. 'It was probably put on when I came into the room,' she said. 'To hide what they were really talking about. You know how women are.'

'No,' Darcy said. 'I don't. But I'm beginning to find out.'

When the girl had gone, Pel turned to Darcy.

'Check on that malaria business of Chenandier's,' he said. 'And the business of being at Dien Bien Phu. It shouldn't be too hard. People who were there are usually proud of it. And what did he mean about Odile? When he stopped so abruptly.'

'He seemed to have remembered something about her, Patron.'

'That's what I thought. Find out what it was. Perhaps she's on drugs or something.'

'She doesn't look as if she is.'

'Find out where she went to school. Who her friends are. What she does with herself. The doctor ought to be able to tell you about her father's malaria. He might even know about Madame Chenandier's lovers. Doctors often do. And while we're at it, let's have someone watch Chenandier. The next-door neighbour, too—Laye. He might turn out to be interesting.'

'How about the Germains?'

Pel frowned. 'Germain's never put in an appearance and, as far as I can make out, isn't likely to, and Madame Germain didn't know the other two families in the lane and didn't want to. They just don't fit into the picture. I think we can forget them.'

'Right, Patron.'

Pel looked at his watch. 'Tomorrow, we'll have another go at Darcq. For the moment, I'm going home.'

'Already?'

Pel avoided his eyes. 'I have a report to get ready for Brisard,' he said. 'He sits on my shoulder like a vulture looking for food.'

Hurrying out of the house, knowing perfectly well that Brisard's report could be delivered by telephone without preparation, what Pel was really looking forward to was another meeting with Didier Darras.

On his way home, he drove on to the Langres road to call in at the Bar de la Frontière where Gervase Darcq made a habit of doing his drinking. It was a dark little place with wine-coloured walls, one painted with an enormous fading sign—BYRRH. Outside were a few shabby chairs under the chestnuts. Men in blue overalls were playing boules, their glasses on a table nearby, and an old woman, her heavy shopping bag on the ground alongside her, sat resting her feet and talking to the proprietress. Next to her, two children sat dangling their toes and listening to an argument developing between two elderly men, who were waving their arms and shouting at each other, curiously without disturbing the scene in the slightest.

The sun had turned to bronze-gold and the shade was rich and deep. There was a smell of dust in the air, mingling with wine and coffee and the whiff of Gauloises. Pel studied the scene for a moment then went inside. The proprietor was leaning on the zinc counter watching the television with an uninterested expression on his face. He turned as Pel appeared.

'Monsieur?'

'Coup de blanc.'

The white wine was poured and Pel sipped it cautiously. It was sharp and acid and he was convinced at once that he'd get indigestion. Gloomily he lit a cigarette then fished out his identity card and laid it down on the counter. The proprietor stared at it.

'Police,' he said. 'I thought you were.'

'Does it show all that much?' Pel asked, startled.

'No.' The proprietor grinned. 'But you're a stranger and we don't get many strangers. You might have been a commercial traveller, of course. But you haven't got the right kind of car and you've got no samples case, so it seemed likely you might be the police.'

'You'd never make a detective,' Pel growled.

'Why not?' It was the proprietor's turn to look disconcerted, as if he prided himself on his shrewdness.

'You jump too much to conclusions.' Pel drew wanly at the cigarette, promising himself it would be the last before his meal—though he knew perfectly well it wouldn't. 'I'm interested in one of your customers,' he said. 'Gervase Darcq.'

'Oh, him.'

'Why, "oh, him"?'

'Well, he's always in trouble, isn't he? Some woman. Some woman's husband. You'd be surprised the sort of people who get up to that sort of thing.' The proprietor nodded to an old man watching the game of boules.

'Him, too?'

'Regularly. He's been threatened more than once.'

Pel's eyebrows lifted.

'It's a dirty old world, isn't it?' the proprietor said.

Pel drew a deep breath. 'Gervase Darcq,' he reminded.

'Yes.' The proprietor frowned heavily to indicate he was concentrating. 'His sister—that woman who was murdered—she was at it, too, wasn't she?'

'At what?'

'What we were talking about.'

'How do you know? Did she come here?'

'No. But he talked about her.'

'What did he say?'

'Nothing much. Just that he was hoping to get money from her. He was always saying that. Especially when he was broke or on the cadge.'

'Did he get money from her recently?'

'Probably.'

'Why do you say that?'

'Well, he was in here the other night with a lot.'

'Which night?'

'Thursday, was it? The night she was killed. That night.'

'How do you know he had a lot of money? Men don't usually spread it out on the counter.'

'Neither does he. He never has enough for that. But that night he did. He was drunk and he started counting it.'

'How much did he have?

'More than I've ever seen him with before. There were several hundreds and fifties.'

'Could you make a guess?'

'About 2,000 frs. Perhaps three. He didn't count it out loud and I was busy, but I keep my eyes open.'

'Yes,' Pel agreed. 'You do. Does Darcq come in here often?'

'He'll be here soon if you'd like to wait.'

Pel finished his wine. 'I have things to do tonight,' he said.

The landlord hitched at his apron. It was stained where his stomach rubbed against the counter.

'Well, you could catch him in the morning,' he said. 'He's in here around seven for a coffee and croissant on his way to work.'

'Every day?'

'Every day that he hasn't been at the booze the night before.'

When Pel reached home, Didier Darras was sitting on the front step. He smiled immediately, and as Pel found himself smiling back, he realised it was something he hadn't done for a long time. It felt odd. As if his face had gone soft.

'Feel like a game of boules?' he asked.

The boy grinned. 'Thought you might like to take me fishing.'

The river was twenty kilometres away and they went in Pel's car which they parked under the trees. There was a line of men along the bank, somnolent over their rods in the sunshine. Everywhere you looked in France—even in Paris under the Pont Neuf—there were fishermen somnolent in the sunshine. A French heaven had to include fishermen in the sunshine. Further along, downstream, there was a small plage with cabins for changing, swings and seesaws, where stout and elderly Frenchmen did callisthenics under the eye of an instructor.

'Wouldn't you prefer to swim?' Pel asked as they sat down among the reeds and put out their rods.

'I'd rather fish.'

'Why?'

'All those kids.'

'Don't you like other children?'

'Not much.'

'Don't you get lonely?'

'I get on all right with me.'

Pel saw what he meant. So did he.

The boy was pulling things from his pocket and laying them on the grass alongside his rod. 'Know anything that'll dissolve chewing gum?' he asked.

'Sorry. Why?'

'I've got some in my pocket. It's all mixed up with string and a pocket knife.' He nodded at a girl hurrying past towards the plage. 'That one's all right,' he observed. 'You ever been married, Monsieur Pel?'

'No.'

'Why not?'

'Never got round to it.'

'How about Tante Annabelle?—Madame Routy.'

Pel shuddered and Didier went on. 'Mind, you'd have to do something about that television, though.'

There was a pause then the boy went on casually. 'You solving any mysteries at the moment, Monsieur Pel?'

'Yes.' Pel hesitated, wondering if young ears would like the sound of murder. 'Somebody was killed,' he said. 'At Aigunay-le-Petit.'

Didier shrugged, indifferent. 'I read about it in the paper. Blood everywhere. I expect she had a boyfriend. Next door neighbour, perhaps.'

Pel nodded. It was an idea.

CHAPTER
TEN

Pel was at the Bar de la Frontière early next day. The morning sun was silver rather than the gold of the previous evening and gave an entirely different quality—joyous instead of calm—to the outlook. The routiers, leaning against their lorries to exchange news and cigarettes, nodded to him as he passed, and the proprietor recognised him at once and gestured with his head for him to go to the end of the zinc counter away from the other customers. Expecting information, Pel followed him away from where his wife was dispensing coffee, croissants and bread. The proprietor gestured again with his head.

'The big chap with the moustache,' he said.

'What about him?'

'He's one.'

'One what?'

The proprietor gave him a disgusted look. 'What we were talking about last night. Goes at it like a ferret.'

Pel stared at the customer in question. 'You must live an entertaining life here,' he said.

The proprietor grinned. 'Not half,' he said. 'Have this on the house. What would you like? Coffee?'

'No. *Coup de blanc*.'

'This time in the morning? You'll get a liver.'

'I need to keep my strength up.'

The proprietor poured the wine and Pel sipped from the glass, frowning and trying hard to avoid lighting a cigarette. He managed to resist for about three minutes, then he sighed and fished out the packet. He had just lit up when Gervase Darcq appeared. He was looking better this time. His face had recovered its colour and he had shaved. He took his coffee and croissant at the bar and Pel saw the proprietor's head move in a faint nod. Darcq turned and saw Pel.

'You looking for me?' he asked.

'Yes.'

Darcq sat down alongside Pel, dipping his croissant into his coffee.

'Again?' he said.

'Yes,' Pel said unemotionally. 'Again.'

'I didn't do it, you know. More like Hervé Chenandier.'

'He thinks *you* did it.'

'He would.'

'There was no love lost between you?'

'That penny-pinching salaud? That salopard? That snake, that Judas, that betrayer, that pimp, that leech, that back-stabber?'

'I take it you don't like him.'

'He thought I was a waster.' Darcq grinned. 'He was right, of course. I am. I always have been. He was always fighting with my sister because she kept slipping me money. He said it was throwing good money after bad.' Darcq grinned once more. 'Once again, he was dead right. It was. I either lost it on the horses or peed it against the wall.'

'You were pretty drunk when we first found you?'

'Yes.'

'I thought you were broke. What did you pay for it all with?'

Darcq frowned as if the question was unexpected and difficult. 'I expect someone lent me some,' he said. 'Or perhaps *she* did.'

'Your sister?'

'Yes.'

'I was in here last night. They said you had a fat roll of notes. The night she was murdered.'

Darcq looked at Pel from the corner of his eye and didn't reply.

'They thought there must have been around 3,000 frs. You laid them out on the zinc and counted them.'

'Someone must have been generous.'

'Who?'

'God knows. I can never remember. That's why I never manage to pay them back.'

'3,000 frs is a generous loan to someone like you. You'd better come clean.'

Darcq frowned again. 'Hang on,' he said. 'I have it. I remember. I put some money on a horse and it came up.'

'How much?'

'Can't remember now. My mind doesn't go back that far.'

'It must have been a good sum. Where did you get it?'

'Merde! How do I know?'

'Where did you put the money on?'

'With Crona. I met one of his runners in a bar in the city.'

'Which one?'

'How do I know? They're in all the bars and so am I.'

'What was the horse?'

'I don't know. I don't keep a list.'

'You mean you've no idea of the name of the horse that won you 3,000 frs? What about the man who took the money? What was *his* name?'

'I can't remember that either.'

'Was it one horse? Or a combination of horses?'

'One. I was lucky.'

'But you can't remember its name?'

'No.'

'I would.' Pel spoke with the deep feeling of someone who *never* won on a horse. 'Especially if I'd won *that* much.'

Because of his visit to the bar, Pel was in his office early. He was thinking about Darcq. He knew he had enough on him to bring him in, but he preferred for the time being to leave him free. He thrust his thoughts aside and decided to take the opportunity to do some work. In fact, he overdid it and when Darcy arrived he was in a bad temper. He had spent hours checking railway timetables, and as they were like gibberish to him, he hadn't enjoyed it. But, since Darcy and Nosjean—even Lagé, Krauss and Misset—hadn't arrived, he had to do the job himself.

He was just about to hurl the timetable across the room in disgust when Darcy appeared. He sat down and lit a cigarette. 'I've been checking the carpark in the Rue Charles-Briffaut, Patron,' he said. 'They know Chenandier and they insist his car *was* there all the time he was in Paris.'

'*All* the time?'

'That's what the attendant said. He knows the car well— a grey Merc like Laye's next door. Côte d'Or number— 9704-QT-21. He's quite prepared to swear.' Darcy glanced pointedly at the timetables. 'What's in your mind, Patron? That he came from Paris on the train, drove out to Aigunay, murdered his wife, returned his car to the carpark, then took the train back to Paris?'

'Yes.' Pel frowned. 'But there must have been enough blood splashed round that room to drown a cat. Yet there's none in his car and no one has it on their clothes.'

'*Could* it have been a tramp, Patron? We're still checking.'

Pel shook his head. 'I think it was somebody cleverer than that. There were no fingerprints and Leguyader thinks whoever did it wore gloves.'

'That's not the way tramps behave,' Darcy said. 'Somebody went prepared.'

As Darcy disappeared, Pel returned to his thankless task of trying to work out alternative routes to and from Paris. In the end, accepting the inevitable, he admitted to himself that it was something he'd never manage to do efficiently and, calling Nosjean, tossed it into his lap instead.

Nosjean backed away like a startled foal, the whites of his eyes showing. 'I don't understand those things, Chief,' he bleated.

'I sympathise with you,' Pel said dryly. 'Neither do I. But somebody's got to do it.'

Nosjean looked gloomy. He felt he was being put on. 'What are we trying to find out?' he asked warily.

'If it's possible some way to get here from Paris and back again in one night. It's not possible direct, but it might be possible via Langres or Châtillon. Check with the railway enquiry office if necessary.'

'Why not try the chap who found that railwayman who was shot?' Nosjean said. 'Barbièry—he's supposed to be an expert, isn't he? He works in the enquiry office, and he also does it for fun.'

Pel looked up. 'You know, Nosjean,' he said, 'sometimes I think you must be a lot brighter than you look.'

Nosjean wasn't being bright. He had a date with his girlfriend that evening and he knew that if he had to hang round the railway enquiry office it might take all day and make him late.

'It's nothing, Patron,' he said with disarming modesty.

Pel decided grudgingly that perhaps some credit should be given for effort. 'Might be worth a try,' he agreed. 'He seemed a reasonable chap. Bit excitable and wanders a bit when he's talking but he knows what he's about when he's dealing with railway timetables. You might also ask him about Giulle while you're at it. They lived next door to each other and he found the body. Kill two birds with one stone.'

Nosjean was looking much happier as he turned away. 'Right, Patron.'

'Just one more thing—' Nosjean stopped '—before you do that, just get on the telephone and try a few jewellers for me. Get that list of the stuff stolen from the Chenandiers' from Darcy and try it on them.'

Nosjean wasn't looking half as happy as he had been. 'It'll take a bit of time, Patron,' he said, seeing his ideas of arriving on time at his girlfriend's whistling down the wind. 'It's supposed to be my night off, too.'

Pel shrugged. 'There's a murder enquiry on,' he pointed out coldly. 'It shouldn't take you long.'

No, Nosjean thought bitterly. Until about midnight, that's all.

Unlike Nosjean, Sergeant Darcy was an opportunist. As he was fond of saying, being careful not to miss an opportunity sometimes caused other opportunities to arise—especially with girls. It was important to take everything seriously.

'Nobody takes *me* seriously,' Nosjean complained.

'Nobody ever takes a detective your age seriously,' Darcy admitted. 'But rest assured, mon brave, one day

they will. Not Pel perhaps. Not God himself. But somebody. Maybe if you have a son, he will. *Maybe*, anyway.'

Making sure he never let slip a chance was a rule Darcy
followed religiously. Which was why his love life was
entirely satisfactory. Nothing was wasted, and now, seeing
an opportunity in front of his nose, he followed his own
rules and snatched at it. In view of Pel's interest in the
possibilities of getting to Paris and back by train, he had
been involved in timing the distance between the station
and Aigunay, and he was just on his way back into the city
when, as he called in the garage in the village for petrol, he
saw Laye's big Mercedes pull in ahead of him and decided it
might be a chance to watch him in action.

Sitting in his car, his face buried in a map, he watched
Laye carefully, noticing that he filled his car himself. The
proprietor's wife was working the pumps and she waved
and called 'Good Morning', but it was Laye who started the
pump and put the nozzle into the neck of the petrol tank.
Then, Darcy noticed, instead of fishing in his wallet for
money, he went into the small glass-walled office where the
telephone was and signed a chit in a small metal dispenser
that held carbon paper for copies. There was what
appeared to be a short interchange of jokes, delivered with
Laye's face close to the proprietor's wife's, then Laye
climbed back into his Mercedes and drove away.

For a moment longer, Darcy watched. The proprietor's
wife was young and, despite her apron, she was attractive
with a good figure, and it set Darcy thinking. His own car
filled, he went into the office to pay and the proprietor's
wife counted out his change and left to attend to another
motorist while Darcy slowly stuffed the notes away. Leaning over the counter, he examined the chit Laye had signed.
It carried the date, his name, the number of litres he'd
had, the price, and his signature. He noticed it was in green
ink.

As the proprietor's wife came back for more change for
her new customer, Darcy produced his badge and gestured
at the slip.

'I'm interested in that,' he said.

The woman shrugged. 'Monsieur Laye. He has an account.'

'Does he always serve himself?'

'But of course. He has a garage, too, so it's all part of the system. On doit se débrouiller. You have to look after yourself.'

'Where is his garage?'

'On the N74. Just beyond Beaune. Orbeaux Brothers. It's his in spite of the name. He has his work done there and only gets petrol here because it's handy for his home.'

Darcy nodded, pushed away his wallet and climbed into his car. Glancing at his watch, he decided he still had plenty of time. He might even stop in Beaune and pick up some wine while he was out there. His girl-friend had a liking for good wine.

Orbeaux Brothers was on the right-hand side of the road. It was said that all the conservatives lived on that side, while all the socialists lived on the other; and that the wine they produced went with them—that on the right rich and full-bodied, that on the left thin and meagre. It was a small set-up and Darcy pretended to be an agent for car accessories. With the elder Orbeaux in Beaune collecting spare parts, it was the young brother who greeted him.

'Accessories?' he said, grinning. 'You've a hope. We make 'em. We're part of the Laye group.'

Darcy pretended to be dismayed at his own lack of perception and got talking about Laye himself.

'It must be all right having your own garage,' he said. 'With the price of things these days. Does he have his car serviced here?'

'Wouldn't you?'

It turned out that Laye was fussy about his car and Orbeaux, who was only twenty, was inclined to be talkative.

'There's always a long list of things he wants doing,' he said. 'Even writes it all out.'

'He does? I don't believe you! Not with a Merc!'

'Well, look.' The boy dug into a cupboard and produced a sheaf of papers held together with a spring clip.

'Time sheets for the mechanos,' he said. 'His list's clipped on as a check.'

Darcy studied the paper. 'Oil, tyres, etc.,' the list said. 'Check exhaust. Rattle in offside door. Doubtful ignition. Reversing light.' Underneath it was Laye's name and his office address.

'Look,' Darcy said. 'I've got to get in touch with him if I can. I might persuade him to take something. Can I keep this? For the address.'

Orbeaux studied the time sheet the slip had been attached to.

'I suppose so,' he said. 'It's all on here. That's only a check.'

'Thanks. In case I don't get hold of him, tell him I called. Jean-Pierre Audubert, Accessories Manoury, Rue Charles-Gilbert, Paris.'

As he drove away, Darcy waved cheerfully and looked at his watch. He just had time to do *one* more check.

When Darcy returned to the Hôtel de Police, Pel had just gone out to his car and was sitting behind the wheel, frowning. One of the civilian clerks was wheeling her bike down the steps. It had a long loaf strapped on the carrier and Pel had just decided that, because of its ubiquitousness, bread ought to be part of the national emblem of France. Crossed baguettes couchant over a bottle of Burgundy.

'Doing a bit of thinking, Patron?' Darcy asked.

'I do from time to time,' Pel said.

'So do I. I wondered if perhaps Chenandier used a hire car to get from the station.'

'And did he?'

'Not from here. At least, nobody around here hired out anything that day to anybody who could have been Chenandier. In fact—' Darcy gestured with his big hand '— even if they had, he'd never have got home in time from the last train—in his own *or* a hired car—to be there when his wife appears to have been killed. I tried it. I timed it. It couldn't be done.'

Pel frowned and Darcy went on cheerfully.

'One other thing—'

'You've been busy!'

'I'm a glutton for punishment. I checked with the family doctor for you. He didn't know Chenandier suffered from malaria. At least he'd never treated him for it. But he *was* at Dien Bien Phu. Everybody knew it, it seems. And, as the doctor said, people who've been in the East learn to live with malaria, and those para boys at DBP *were* a tough lot.'

Pel nodded and reached for the ignition key. Darcy's hand stopped him.

'One last thing, Patron,' he said. 'That assignation note we found in Madame Chenandier's handbag. I've found out whose writing it is.'

'Go on. Whose?'

'Chap next door. Laye.'

Pel's eyebrows lifted. 'How did you manage that masterpiece?'

'Sheer luck. I happened to follow him into the garage at Aigunay for petrol and I saw his name on the chit.' Darcy pushed a slip of paper through the window. 'That's his writing—instructions to Orbeaux Brothers for servicing his car. You'll see it's the same as in the note found in the handbag. The paper's the same too—torn off the same pad, I imagine.'

'That's good, Darcy.'

Darcy smiled. 'I'm sweating on promotion,' he pointed out.

'I shouldn't,' Pel said. 'You're bound to do something stupid tomorrow.'

CHAPTER ELEVEN

When Pel reached the office the following morning the
reporters were waiting outside.

'Come on, Inspector,' Sarrazin urged. 'You haven't told
us a thing yet.'

'I've noticed that.' Pel waved the newspaper at him.
'From the fairy stories I've been reading.'

He agreed to meet them and gave them a few details—
about the murder weapon and the estimated time of
death—but little else.

'It's not much,' Sarrazin complained.

'Knowing you lot,' Pel said, 'you'll be able to write a
novel on it.'

He hadn't escaped yet, however, because Judge Brisard
was on the telephone from the Palais de Justice within a
minute, as if he'd been lying in ambush. He sounded
irritated and for a change came to the point at once.

'We don't seem to be making much headway, Pel,' he
said, and Pel didn't fail to notice the absence of his title.

'We?' he said sharply.

Brisard coughed in embarrassment. 'A figure of speech.
You, of course. This thing's been going on for weeks now.'

'Days,' Pel corrected.

'Either way, I've got the Director of Prosecutions on my
neck wanting to know when we're going to arrest someone.
When will it be?'

'When we find someone,' Pel said.

Brisard's voice became shrill. 'Surely you've formed an
opinion by now?' he said.

'I always keep an open mind.'

'Is that a good idea?'

'In the interests of justice, yes. And not only in the
interests of justice. But also in the interests of the department, which might be embarrassed if I start accusing all the

wrong people. Also, come to that, in mine, too, because I've no doubt the department wouldn't allow itself to be made the scapegoat if I did get the wrong one.'

Brisard was silent for a moment. 'We have to make some sort of showing,' he insisted. 'Surely there's someone you can set up for me to question? Perhaps I could bring out something you've missed.'

Pel almost laughed. 'Give me a little longer,' he said. 'We mustn't rush this thing.'

Brisard paused again, intimidated as he always was by Pel's lack of co-operation. 'Sometimes, Pel,' he said bitterly. 'I think you don't like me.'

When Darcy came in he seemed full of beans again.

'Well,' Pel said. 'What have *you* been up to? Apart, that is, from popping in and out of bed with various young women.'

Darcy looked innocent. 'I'm treading carefully at the moment,' he said. 'This one's a new one and she probably has a husband who's a weight-lifter.'

'Well, you've obviously got that side of your life well buttoned up,' Pel said sarcastically. 'How about the side that concerns the department?'

Darcy grinned. 'Making headway, Chief,' he said. 'I'm expecting to pick up something about the daughter today. I've arranged to ring her old school. It's a private one. Expensive. In Switzerland. I noticed she left at the age of fifteen without taking her baccalaureat, and finished her education here. I wondered why. One final thing: the lab report. They found one small bloodstain in the bedroom. Right by that open drawer. Leguyader also noticed two more on the stairs. Tiny marks, as though someone had some blood on their shoe and trod it upstairs.'

'The girl?'

'That's what I wondered.'

Pel nodded, offering no praise. 'Where's Nosjean?' he asked.

'Doing leg work round the jewellers. Something you set him on, he says.'

'He should have finished by now.' Pel waved Darcy away. 'Go and ring your school,' he said. 'I've a few people to see.'

The two Laye children were just leaving for the university when Pel pulled up his car alongside them.

'Give you a lift?' he asked.

The boy accepted readily, the girl, Anne-Marie, less so. They were at different departments and he dropped the boy first at the Faculté de Médecine. As the door closed, the girl sat quietly alongside Pel, almost warily.

'I don't mind walking the rest of the way,' she said.

'No trouble,' Pel said. 'It's on my route. I've got a call to make before going to headquarters.'

The girl said nothing and Pel drove in silence for a while.

'Father usually give you a lift into town?' he asked.

She gestured with her shoulders. 'He's always too busy.'

'Doing what?'

'Business. Going to work. Coming from work.'

Pel drove in silence for a while before he spoke again. 'Don't you get on with your father?' he asked. 'Some children don't.'

She shifted uneasily alongside him. 'No, I don't.' Her voice was thin and defiant.

Pel nodded. 'I thought not,' he said. 'When I was talking to you all the other day, you got up and went out of the room. Abruptly. Any special reason for that?'

She kept her eyes down. 'No.'

'I'd just asked your parents if they knew Madame Chenandier. Your mother said no. Then your father said he'd hardly ever exchanged a single word.'

'He would.'

'Then you got up and walked out. Why?'

'Because I felt like it.'

'I thought for a moment it might be because you didn't agree with what your father said.'

'I don't.'

Pel let her brood in silence for a while before he went on.

'Were you at home the night Madame Chenandier was murdered?' he asked.

'No. I was at a party.'

'And your brother?'

'At the same party.'

'Were you there all the time?'

'Yes. So I couldn't have done it, could I?'

'No, you couldn't,' Pel agreed. 'Did your brother stay there all the time, too?'

'Yes. So he couldn't either, could he?'

'How about your mother?'

'Out playing bridge. She's always playing bridge. All day and all night.'

'Where?'

'In Dijon. Someone with an apartment opposite the palace. She goes there a lot. They're obsessed with it.'

There had been a traffic accident on the corner of the Rue de Mirande and the Boulevard Jeane-d'Arc and the two car owners were in the centre of the road exchanging addresses and insults, while a traffic policeman, his képi on the back of his head, was glaring through his dark spectacles, blowing shrill symphonies on his whistle and gesturing at the traffic to keep moving. They had to wait until the congestion cleared, and Pel glanced at the girl who was sitting silently alongside him without saying a word. With a final glare and a last peremptory swing of his white baton, the policeman got the cars moving again and Pel began to edge forward. Conscious of the girl's hostility, he came back gently to his questioning.

'How did you get to this party you went to?' he asked.

'We got a lift with friends,' she said. 'We walked to the Rue Clément-Rémy and they picked us up there.'

'Did you notice anything unusual in the Chemin-de Champ-Loups when you left? Any strangers? That sort of thing.'

'There was a car in the lane.'

'Yes, I know. It was your father's.'

'No, not that one. I knew that was there. This was another. One I'd never seen before.'

Pel looked quickly at her. 'You sure about that?'

'Of course. There are only three houses in the lane and I know all the cars that belong to them or visit them.'

'What sort of car was it?'

'I don't know. A good-sized car, that's all I know.'

'Colour?'

'Black or dark blue.'

'Where was it?'

'Down the lane. Well down.'

His mind on what she was saying, Pel swung the car into the Boulevard Gabriel, found himself face to face with a Nicolas lorry that came from nowhere, avoided it with difficulty and settled back in his seat, convinced his nerves were shattered. It was quite a while before he went on.

'Where was your father that evening?' he asked.

Anne-Marie Laye shrugged. 'He wasn't in when I left. He probably didn't come in until late. He often didn't when my mother played bridge.'

'Did he know she was playing bridge?'

'She told him when he came home for lunch. He said he'd eat in the city.'

'Did he?'

'I shouldn't think so.'

'What do you mean by that?'

'What he got up to when my mother was playing bridge is anybody's guess.'

Pel swung the car towards the Faculté de Lettres and stopped. 'What *did* he get up to?' he asked.

She made no attempt to get out. 'What do most men get up to?' she said.

'Well, tell me. What?'

'I think he had a bit of fluff.'

'Who was she?'

'I don't know. I can guess, though.'

'Would you like to guess for me?'

'No.'

'Someone you know. Someone close to home?'

The girl stared at him then she shook her head. 'I don't know,' she said.

'Or don't want to tell me?'

Her eyes sparkled with tears and Pel decided it was a sad world, with devious, dishonest parents making devious, dishonest children. How many other children were there in the world who failed to get on with their parents? Or was it a case of parents failing to get on with their children? Perhaps it was the dishonesty of the age. Perhaps if he'd had children of his own—

He stopped dead as his thoughts began to run away with him. He was nobody to criticise. He'd never even had the courage to marry.

'I could make you tell me, you know,' he said gently. 'But I won't. Did your mother know what your father got up to?'

The girl's shoulders sagged. 'There was talk of a divorce once. But it all died down.'

'Why?'

'It seemed to come right again. For a while, anyway. Then it started again.'

Pel paused. 'Was he friendly with Madame Chenandier?'

There was a sudden stony silence then the girl answered in a sharp breathless voice. 'That's a mild word for what they did.' She spoke with all the harsh disillusionment of adolescence, as if she'd suddenly discovered that all the romance she'd imagined existed had changed to harsh crudity, as if the fairy stories she'd believed in as a child had given place to cynical reality.

'How do you know all this?'

'I saw them. More than once.'

'How?'

'From my bedroom. I don't think they ever knew I could see from the corner of my window.'

Her bitterness was sharp, even shocking, and Pel paused to let her recover a little. 'Do you think he was there the night Madame Chenandier was murdered?' he asked eventually.

The girl hesitated then opened the car door and climbed out as if she intended to ignore him. Then she changed her mind. 'You'd better ask him, hadn't you?' she said.

'Yes,' Pel agreed. 'Perhaps I had.'

*   *   *

Laye's office was behind the Palace near the pedestrian precinct. A grey Mercedes that Pel recognised as Laye's was parked outside. He studied it cautiously, almost as if it might spit in his eye. There was a brief case on the seat, a set of maps, a few folders for Laye's firm and one, he noticed, for Luxe Hire Cars, Paris, half-covered by a navy-blue anorak with a zip front and zips on the pockets.

Deep in thought, he lit a cigarette, unaware of what he was doing, realised as the match burned his fingers what he'd done and took the cigarette from his mouth in disgust. He was about to throw it away when he remembered how much they cost, so, sadly, he smoked it half-way down then tossed it aside, trying to believe that for once he'd fought the craving. Climbing a set of stairs, he found himself facing a door marked 'Laye et Cie.'

'Monsieur Laye?' he said, pushing inside.

The girl behind the counter pulled a face. 'Not possible,' she said shortly. 'He's busy.'

'Not too busy to see me.'

'I think he is.'

Pel produced his identification card and her expression changed. 'I'll tell him you're here.'

Laye's desk was as full of gadgets, panels, buttons and lights as the dashboard of a Boeing 747 and he was answering two telephones at once when Pel appeared in his office. Without stopping talking, he gestured with his head to a chair. As Pel sat down, he brought the conversation to a close like a maestro bringing a symphony orchestra safely through the climax of a major work, and slammed the two telephones down together.

'Pretty busy, Inspector,' he said. 'Hope it won't take long.'

'Shouldn't,' Pel said.

The telephone went and Laye was just reaching for it when Pel put his hand on it. 'That is, if we're not interrupted,' he said.

'I have my business to attend to.'

'So have I.'

Laye shrugged and, switching on an inter-com, spoke to

the girl outside. 'I'm in to no one, Geneviève,' he said. 'Not until I tell you.'

He flipped the switch and sat back in his chair. 'Very well, Inspector,' he said. 'What do you want? I hope it won't take long. With an office, a car accessory factory, a welding firm at Bazay, a garage, and five car-hire firms, I'm pretty busy.'

'So am I,' Pel pointed out.

Laye sighed and made an effort to sound interested. 'Have you found out anything yet?'

'Not much,' Pel admitted. 'I'm still sniffing around.'

'And me? Why do you want me?'

'Someone was in the lane outside the Chenandier house the night of the murder,' Pel said. 'I wonder if you saw him.'

'Him?'

'It was a man. The gardener saw him.'

Laye's eyes flickered. 'Why would I see him?'

'You were probably at home.'

'I don't think so.'

'Your car was in the lane. The gardener saw it. Drawn up under the trees near your house.'

'Doesn't mean I was there.'

'You entered your house at roughly the time the murder was taking place.'

'Who says?'

'Never mind who says.'

Laye's face darkened. 'Are you suggesting—?'

'I'm suggesting nothing,' Pel said. 'I asked if you saw anyone.'

'I saw no one because I wasn't there.'

'Where were you?'

'I think I walked down the lane a little. I seem to remember having a headache. It had been a tough day. We get them occasionally. You must have them yourself.'

To Pel, all days were tough days. When Madame Routy was difficult about the late film, sometimes the nights were tough as well.

He nodded. 'Any proof of this walk?'

'No. I'd be alone, of course.'

'Do you often take walks when you get home?'

'After a bad day, it helps me to settle myself before I go in. Then I don't take it out of my wife.'

'Your wife was playing bridge that day.'

'Was she?'

'Yes. She'd told you. You came home for lunch and she told you then.'

'Then perhaps I *thought* she was in and *wanted* to be in a good mood.'

'Do you always try to please your wife?'

'Of course.'

'Does she suspect that you have girlfriends?'

Laye's head jerked up. 'What do you mean?'

'I think you know.'

'Who told you that? My daughter, I suppose.'

'I asked her.'

'Why?'

'As a check. I got it from another source—two, as a matter of fact. If you don't want your affairs to be found out, you shouldn't write notes. It isn't hard to check handwriting. Madame Chenandier was one, wasn't she?'

Laye looked angrily at his hands then he shrugged. 'Yes,' he said. 'She was.'

'Mistress?'

'No. Just—well—she was a highly-sexed woman, and after twenty years of marriage marital sex becomes—well—' Laye shrugged and became silent.

'When did you go and see her? When your wife was out playing bridge and Chenandier was in Paris?'

'I suppose so.'

'It was unfortunate for you that your wife was playing bridge and Chenandier was in Paris when his wife was killed.'

'Look,' Laye said, suddenly agitated, 'I didn't do it.'

'Can you prove it?'

'No. Except that—' Laye stopped. 'I suppose it was the gardener who saw me. I knew Chenandier was in Paris and I'd slipped her that note. I'd been going to see her when I saw the gardener appear carrying his damned fork. I hid in the trees. I thought he hadn't spotted me. I waited for a long time then I went for a walk down the lane and came back and tried again. But there was someone already there.'

'What time was this?'

'About 11.00 p.m. by this time.'

'Did you see a car in the lane? A car that you didn't recognise.'

'Yes, I did.'

'What sort was it?'

'I don't know.'

'Colour?'

'I don't know that either. Just a car. Dark-coloured.'

'You have a Mercedes. That's the sort of car a keen motorist would have. Are you one?'

'I suppose so.'

'I'd have thought a keen motorist would have noticed the make of a strange car he saw near his house.'

'Well, I didn't.' Laye frowned, irritated by the questioning. 'It was too far away. Right at the end of the lane where it narrows into a footpath. Parked under the trees. I was never near enough to see what sort of car it was in the dark.'

'I thought you went down there. For a walk. Before going in to your wife.'

Laye gestured. 'No,' he admitted. 'Actually, I just hung about in the lane, waiting for whoever it was to come out.'

'Who was this person? Do you know?'

'No. I could just hear voices. Once even a scream. They seemed to be quarrelling. I could hear them above that stereo she plays.'

'What did you do?'

'What would *you* do? I went home. It seemed safer. My wife was out.'

'When she returned did you tell her that you'd heard quarrelling next door.'

'No.'

'Or what you'd been doing?'

Laye eyed him with his calm yellow eyes. 'Would you?' he said.

*   *   *

Leaving Laye's office, Pel went back to headquarters, and was studying the duty lists in the outer office when Nosjean appeared, all bright-eyed and eager.

'Well, spit it out,' Pel said. 'Before you burst.'

'I checked the train, Patron,' he said. 'There isn't any way at all of getting here from Paris apart from the usual trains.'

'Who did you ask?'

'The station. They weren't very helpful.'

'They never are. Why didn't you ask Barbièry? I thought you were going to see him.'

'He wasn't on duty.'

'Well, go and see him now. At home, if necessary.'

'I'm still checking the jewellers.' Nosjean's protest was like the bleating of a shorn lamb.

'You should have finished that by now,' Pel said, unmoved.

Nosjean flapped his hands in desperation. 'They don't like discussing these things on the telephone, they say. They say crooks try it on occasionally to find out what they've got. I'm having to do it all personally.'

'Well, what in the name of the Great Lord God of Stresses of Strains are you making such a fuss about?'

Nosjean swallowed and managed to control himself. 'I'm not making a fuss, Chief.'

'You mean you can fit it all in?'

Nosjean was a born innocent. 'Easily, Chief,' he gritted.

'Good.' Pel looked up and smiled his death's head grin. 'Misset's wife's baby's arrived and he's got to have time off. You'd better also take over the search across the stream again for the time being.'

'Chief—!' As Nosjean realised what he'd done, his protest came in a cry of anguish.

But Pel wasn't even listening. 'You've got a couple of men to do the work,' he pointed out. 'All you've got to do is keep an eye on them.'

Nosjean sighed. It had been his intention to slip away early.

'Had you something planned?' Pel asked.

'Yes, Patron. I was hoping to see my girl.'

'Darcy says you should never encourage them to be demanding.'

'She doesn't get the chance to be demanding,' Nosjean said bitterly. 'I never get to see her. She's beginning to wonder if I'm keen. She says she needs security.'

'Security's a habit,' Pel said. 'Like insecurity. If you hurry, you ought to get back before bedtime. You could slip round and see her for ten minutes.'

'I suppose I couldn't tackle it in the morning, could I, Patron?'

Pel didn't turn a hair. 'No,' he said. 'You couldn't.'

Nosjean headed for the door. 'I thought I couldn't,' he admitted.

Darcy appeared with his notebook in his hand. 'You'll drive that kid out of the Force,' he observed.

'Or make a policeman of him,' Pel said. 'I've got a job for you.'

Darcy affected a disbelieving look, and Pel scowled.

'Go and see Laye,' he said. 'Arrange to have his clothes checked by the lab. And do it discreetly. I don't want to start a divorce but I want them all checked. He'll agree, I think.'

'Right.'

'Did you check Darcq's story of his bet?'

'Yes. With Crona, the bookmaker. Darcq didn't put anything on there.'

'Couldn't he have put it on anywhere else?'

'He might. But he picked the wrong day to win 3,000. Crona said there were no big winners. It was all short odds. He'd have had to put on at least 100 frs to end up with 3,000 that night. And I dare bet he hadn't got anything like that much. It was just before pay day.'

Pel nodded. 'What about the other checks?'

'Nothing from the tails.'

'What about the laundries?'

'Nothing, Chief. I've checked them. *And* the cleaners. Nothing there either. Nothing's been handed in that re-

motely resembles the clothes we're looking for. I thought I
was on to it for a minute when I found a pair of bloodstained
trousers at a cleaners in the Rue Henri-Lapointe. But they
belonged to a butcher who'd caught his thigh with his own
cleaver. I also checked the dustbin people. They saw
nothing either.'

Pel looked at Darcy. Considering the time he'd wasted,
he seemed remarkably cheerful. 'All right,' he said. 'Stop
looking like the mother and father of God and tell me what
else you've got. You've obviously found something to
make up for all the things you didn't turn up.'

Darcy gestured and leaned back in his chair. 'I've been in
touch with the school,' he said. 'You remember we discovered Odile left rather abruptly at the age of fifteen. I found
out why.'

'Well? What do you want, spotlights?'

Darcy turned a page of his notebook—slowly, because
he believed in making Pel wait.

'She attacked one of the staff,' he said profoundly.

'A pity more people don't,' Pel snorted. 'I often felt like
it when I was a boy. What was it for?'

'The woman had been needling her. You know what
she's like. Awkward. A bit lost and wet. I imagine she
wasn't very bright or very popular either. It was in a
cookery class. It was one of *those* schools. All the nicest
young ladies, and they were taught all the right things.
Never mind the baccalaureat, so long as they could sing and
play the piano and knew how many courses to serve when
their husband's boss came home.'

'For the love of God, spit it out!'

Darcy smiled. 'Seems she was about as good at cooking
as she was at everything else, and this particular mistress
was always after her. Eventually she upped and clubbed her
with a rolling pin.'

'Fairly conventional weapon,' Pel said. 'For a woman.'

'Apparently, she was trying to hammer her head flat
when she was dragged off. The next day her parents were
sent for and she left.'

'Did they tell the police?'

'It wasn't one of those schools.'

'Probably doesn't mean a thing,' Pel said disconcertingly.

'Patron, if she bashed this mistress, she probably also bashed her mother.'

'And probably she didn't, too. Find out anything more?'

'The school doctor examined her. He decided she was a hysterical type.'

'Is he a psychiatrist?'

'No. Just a school doctor.'

'Then he probably doesn't know a thing about it.'

Darcy eyed him. Pel was obviously in a bad mood. 'One thing I like about you, Patron,' he said. 'You're so encouraging.'

CHAPTER
TWELVE

The city sweltered in the heat. Even up on the slopes of the north, where you could get the breeze, there was no relief. The tar bubbled in the road and the farmers were beginning to complain about lack of water for their cattle. The Hôtel de Police grew more like a greenhouse every day and everybody was asking why it was that modern designers used so much glass—especially in an area where sunshine was by no means unknown.

Cars left in car parks developed seats that were impossible to sit on. Mothers nagged at their children for no other reason than that it was too hot, and at Lignon a baker gave his wife a black eye for the same reason. In Darnay a bank cashier was worrying that an excess of affection provoked by the heat had landed her in trouble, because she and her boyfriend had made love the previous evening and they hadn't been very careful. And in Talant, a young man wearing a shabby red track-suit with broken zips bearing the word 'Toulouse' across the back, sat in his Deux

Chevaux opposite a supermarket brooding over the fact
that the supermarket, which he'd noticed backed on to an
empty yard that wasn't overlooked, would be an easy place
to break into. The word 'Toulouse' on his back meant
nothing at all because he'd never played for Toulouse at
anything. He lacked the energy and will to go in for sport
and he was on drugs, anyway, and always in need of money.
The supermarket, he felt, would solve all his financial
worries for a time.

The vagrants, alcoholics, drug addicts and known nuts
had been checked but, since there were no unexpected
fingerprints in the Chenandier house, it seemed to rule
them out at once; and in any case, to a man they all had
alibis, having been curled up in lodging houses, pleading to
get a bottle, or sleeping one off. As suspects, the vagrants,
alcoholics, drug addicts and known nuts were a dead loss.

There was one other line to follow but Pel was far from
keen. Not because he wasn't meticulous at his job; just,
quite simply, because he didn't want to go to Paris—
especially in a heat wave.

He loathed the metropolis. It was too busy and too noisy,
smelled too much of hot oil and petrol fumes, and there
were so many Americans there these days it looked like the
fifty-first state of the Union. There were also students
everywhere you looked—all hairy and hot and a lot of them
not very clean—and tourists all down the Champs Elysées
and jamming the bateaux mouches until they bulged at the
seams. Pel preferred Dijon any time.

'Do you good to have a break, Chief,' Darcy encouraged.

Pel shuddered. 'All those people,' he said.

'For God's sake, Patron, there are people here!'

'Different people. French people.'

'Why not go and enjoy yourself? Have a few nights out
on the town. Have a good meal.'

'I can get a good meal here. A good Burgundian meal.'

'Find a woman then. It'll relax you.'

Pel stared at Darcy, looking about as relaxed as a lion
tamer in the Cirque d'Hiver going solo for the first time.

'It'll do you good, Chief.' Darcy grinned. 'You're beginning to look as if there's been a death in the family and some people actually manage to enjoy that sort of thing, you know.'

Pel thought briefly of unmentionable sins. Sometimes his loins ached and he felt as eager as a buck rabbit, but he'd spent so many years backing away from women he felt he no longer had much about him to attract them.

He sat in a soured frame of mind all the way north and left the train literally cringing at the noise of the city. Dumping his bag at a hotel, he went out immediately to eat before it was too late, his mind full of Darcy's advice and half-wondering what bestial things he might do to pass the evening. But his mood was as lively as a graveyard and when he had one apéritif too many to cheer himself up, instead it only darkened the horizon even more, so that he drank an extra carafe of wine with his meal for a lift and ended up feeling like a Legionaire's farewell to his mother.

When he woke next morning, his brains felt as if they were slopping about inside his head every time he moved and someone was trying to kick his way out of his skull. Sadly, he stuffed himself with bismuth pills in the hope they'd help him recover and elected to get on with the job as fast as he could so he could go home.

Just for luck he decided to check the Hotel Meurice. It had a faded Second Empire look about it, redolent of dubious weekends and intimate dinners, and the pale green walls were plastered with theatre adverts—for the Lido, the Moulin Rouge, the Crazy Horse—and for tours to Versailles and Fontainebleau. The clerk was on the telephone when he arrived and he finally slammed it down with the air of a Napoleon after Austerlitz. He seemed to have won a major battle against someone in need of a room.

The visit was a waste of time. There was no doubt that Chenandier had spent his week in Paris there. His name was in the register and they even remembered the urgency with which he'd left. His movements also checked exactly with what he'd said. He'd dined out every evening but Friday when he'd stayed in the hotel. Pel's temples ached and he was disappointed because he'd been hoping to catch him out in a lie.

'What about breakfast that morning?' he asked, his elbow on the counter, his hand holding the side of his head in case it dropped off.

The clerk stared at him. 'Friday?'

'Yes, Friday. The day he left.'

'I don't know, Monsieur.' The clerk shrugged. 'I didn't see him. But he might have breakfasted out. He sometimes did.'

'Is the hotel door closed at night?'

'Yes, Monsieur. Locked about 1.30.'

'Until when?'

'6.00 in the morning. Anybody coming in has to ring. The porter had a quiet night.'

'So Monsieur Chenandier must have been in?'

'He must have been. In fact, I saw him Friday morning early, myself. Here in the hall. He'd been out for a news-paper and was complaining that the kiosk hadn't got his usual one—a strike or something—and he'd had to buy something different.'

Pel took a deep breath. 'What time did he leave?' he asked.

The clerk considered. 'Late. That night, when the story was in the papers. He rang down from his room for his bill and said he had to leave in a hurry. We had it ready when he appeared and he left in a taxi we'd called for him. He was in such a hurry he almost left his suitcase behind. It was only a small one—enough for a couple of shirts, a change of underwear, and perhaps a light suit—so it was easy to overlook. He had a brief-case, of course, and a small black case.' The clerk frowned. 'No, he didn't have the small black case. I remember distinctly. I helped him into the taxi and put his luggage in with him. There were just the two. I must have been mistaken. I thought he had three when he came—a small black case as well.' The clerk frowned. 'But he couldn't have. Unless he put it in the taxi himself and I didn't notice.'

*   *   *

Names, addresses and telephone numbers scrawled in his notebook, Pel took a taxi to the Bobino off the Rue de la Gaiété in Montparnasse. The office was open and he introduced himself and laid Chenandier's ticket stub in front of the manager.

'Was that issued here?' he asked.

The manager was inclined to be sarcastic. 'It has our name on it.'

'I'd still like to be sure.'

'Then, yes, Monsieur. It was.'

'When was it issued?'

The manager indicated the date. 'Then, Monsieur.'

'You sure?'

'Had to be. Every ticket's dated for the day of the performance it covers.'

'Have you any idea whom it was issued to?'

'None at all.'

'Would the usherette remember if the seat was occupied?'

'I shouldn't think so for a minute. It's almost a week ago. She probably doesn't even remember last night. We don't pick them for their ability to do mental arithmetic.'

The manager was quite right. When Pel found the usherette she turned out to be elderly, indifferent and blank-faced. Blank-minded, too, Pel decided, wishing his headache would go.

The booking office and the usherette at the Humeur proved to be exactly the same and, returning to the hotel, Pel sat on the bed and, pulling his notebook out, decided to try Luxe Hire Cars, Laye's firm. It was a shot in the dark but he half-hoped it might turn something up.

It did, but not about Chenandier.

The clerk at Luxe Cars was a brisk young man with a beard who wore padded shoulders so wide they seemed to hang down to his elbows. His name was Jean-Jacques Mille and he seemed to be well on top of the job.

'No,' he said firmly. 'No Monsieur Chenandier's been in this office in the last fortnight.' He jabbed a spatulate finger at the hiring book in front of him. 'It'd be there if he had. You tried Jacques Naboulet Hire?'

'No. Should I?'

'I wouldn't. They're not organised. Mind, I'm not surprised, with that dame they employ. How can you run a business when the clerk makes a habit of getting laid by the customers?'

'Is that what happens?'

'Yes.'

Pel paused, lit a cigarette and offered one to Mille. 'Where do your hire cars go to?' he asked.

Mille shrugged. 'Mostly local. Some chap who wants to impress a girl. Somebody whose car's broken down. Mostly short distances.'

'What about last Thursday night?'

Jean-Jacques Mille perused his book. 'Just one long-distance. Kid by the name of Berthelo hired a car to take his elderly father to Rennes.'

'And did he?'

Mille looked at his book. 'The mileage's right,' he said. 'So I suppose he did. He drove himself. It was one of our big Peugeots. The green one. That's a very fashionable colour at the moment, you know. British racing green, it's called. Not that the British have a racing team at the moment. They can't afford a racing wheelbarrow.'

Pel had a feeling he was getting nowhere. He tried a desperate last shot. 'Know Monsieur Laye?'

Mille's eyebrows rose. 'Of course. He's my boss. Well, one of them. The top one.'

'Ever come in here?'

'Sometimes. End of the financial year. If there are problems. That sort of thing.'

'On his own?'

'Usually. But not always. Sometimes he's with—' the clerk's expression changed. He leaned across the counter to Pel. 'Here, is *she* his wife—this Chenandier you're asking about?'

Pel blinked. His luck seemed to have changed. 'Is she?' he asked.

'Aigunay-le-Petit? In Burgundy?'

'That's where *my* Chenandier comes from.'

Mille smoothed his beard. 'He came in with her sometimes.'

'Laye did?'

'Occasionally. I know her well. She uses us when she comes to Paris.'

'I don't think she will any more,' Pel said. 'Did she come in often?'

'No. Not often.'

'Where did they go?'

'I don't know. You don't ask the boss where he's taking his own cars—or his girlfriends.'

'And you? Did you ever have occasion to drive her anywhere?'

'Once.'

'What happened?'

'What do you mean, what happened?'

Pel stared blank-faced at Mille. 'I mean, what happened?'

Mille shrugged and grinned. 'Well, she—well, you know—she was one of those.'

'She made passes at you?'

'I'll say.'

'And you?'

Mille shrugged, suddenly cautious. 'I've got a girl.'

CHAPTER
THIRTEEN

Sergeant Nosjean was at Aigunay-le-Petit, sniffing round in the fields across the stream from the back of the houses in the Chemin de Champ-Loups when Pel arrived back from Paris.

Nosjean felt weary, because *he*'d had a bad night, too.

He'd been to Marsonnay to see Barbièry, the timetable
expert, as Pel had suggested, and found he wasn't in. On
the way back his car had broken down so that, already late
for his date, he'd taken a taxi home. It had cost him a
fortune and he'd been too late, anyway, because his girl had
already gone out in a huff, and when he'd enquired at the
office about getting his money back on expenses, he'd been
informed he should have used a bus.

Now, searching the fields beyond the Chenandier house,
he was suffering from acute depression. The long grass hid
all the usual rubbish you found in fields in summer: Signs of
picnics. Paper. Old bread. Plastic containers. Used con-
traceptives. From the number of those, you'd have thought
that people spent every minute of their lives going at it like
ferrets, though, judging by the number of evenings Nosjean had to work, it seemed it was never going to be *his* luck
to need one.

However, he *had* found a can in the bottom of the hedge
that smelled as if it had contained paraffin; and among the
withered grass on the edge of the field, the remains of a fire,
its ashes pasty grey after the recent rains, which at least
seemed to indicate it had been burning before or during the
night of the Chenandier murder, because there'd been no
rain since.

Deciding to take a closer look, he was poking about with
a stick when he came up with a small charred object which
he studied carefully before stuffing it into a plastic bag. He
felt sure Pel would only sneer at it, but at least he wouldn't
be able to complain that he hadn't been thorough. Poking
about a little more, he found two or three welded lumps of
plastic and decided that perhaps he'd better keep them,
too.

Then, trying to think ahead to all the questions Pel would
be certain to ask him, he walked slowly round the remains
of the fire. It lay in a small hollow surrounded by willows
and he got one of the uniformed men to stand beside it
while he went to the Langres road and then the Chemin de
Champ-Loups.

'What are you up to, Sergeant?' The policeman was

grinning, and obviously considered Nosjean was still wet behind the ears.

'Just trying to think of everything,' Nosjean said huffily.

The policeman continued to grin, so Nosjean retaliated by indicating the petrol can. 'Better get that down to the finger-print boys,' he said.

This time it was the policeman's turn to frown. It was a hot afternoon and it wasn't at all unpleasant there under the trees, while it was a long walk back to the station and a longish drive in the heat to the city. He didn't fancy it at all.

'Now?' he said.

Nosjean noticed that his smile had vanished. 'Yes,' he said triumphantly. 'Now. There might be something on it.'

As the policeman disappeared, grumbling, Nosjean noticed he was being watched from the edge of the dip by the Chenandier girl. She had large, anguished eyes that gave her face a startled vulnerable look. Her skin had a sallow meridional appearance, but she was slim and her figure wasn't bad, and he saw she wasn't wearing a brassiere because he could see the shape of her breasts quite clearly through the T-shirt she wore, and they were full and firm.

'You still looking for clues?' she asked shyly.

Nosjean blushed. He blushed at almost everything and it bothered him in front of girls. 'That's my job,' he said.

She edged a little closer, moving with a curiously humble manner, a little like a spaniel that expected to be scolded, and, looking at her again, Nosjean decided she wasn't half as bad as Darcy had suggested. As appealing as a pile of sand, Darcy had said, but Darcy went in for flashy pieces with bleached hair and *his* tastes and Nosjean's tastes were very different.

Odile seemed on the point of joining Nosjean in the hollow but seemed to think better of it. She moved awkwardly, all arms and legs, as though she couldn't make up her mind what to do, and it occurred to Nosjean, as it had occurred to him the first time she'd approached him in the garden when he'd found Pel's cigarette end, that she was lonely and desperately anxious to talk to him.

'It was my mother who was killed,' she said.

She was trying terribly hard to make conversation and, because he was bored, Nosjean had no objection. 'Yes,' he said. 'I'm sorry.'

'Do they know who did it yet?'

'Not yet,' Nosjean said. 'But we shall before long.'

She was silent for a while, studying him. There was a lost, desperate look on her face that Nosjean couldn't understand.

'It would be terrible if it were someone we all knew, wouldn't it?' she said.

'I suppose so,' Nosjean agreed. 'But I don't suppose it will be.' He paused. 'You're not on your own in the house, are you?'

'No. There's a housekeeper and my father. He's come back now.'

Nosjean nodded, wishing his own girl would sometimes be as forthcoming as this one appeared to wish to be. He was young and he was in love. For years his heart had spent its time sliding around under his shirt like aspic on a hot plate every time he met a new girl. He'd thought it was steady at last, however, because for two months he'd been going with a typist who worked in a solicitor's office and his heart was making a brave effort to move like a metronome. Unfortunately, his girl seemed to regard police work as unprofitable, badly paid and possessing no future, and to his fury spent all her time telling him about the young solicitors who worked with her.

'Have you been a policeman long?' Odile asked in a breathless sort of way.

'A fair time,' Nosjean said. 'But not a sergeant. That's fairly new.'

'Oh! Is it difficult?'

'Sometimes.' Nosjean tried to look determined. 'Sometimes it's a bit tricky. At least it is to me. I'm no Maigret. Not yet anyway.'

He'd been trying to make her smile because her expressionlessness worried him.

But her face didn't change and he hurried on. 'It'll come easier when I've had more practice,' he said.

'It must be very interesting.'

This was a new attitude to Nosjean and he felt pleased and flattered. 'Well—' he was just about to launch into a treatise on detective work when he saw Pel beyond the stream and decided he'd better look as if he were busy.

'Look,' he said. 'My boss's just arrived. I'd better get on with it.'

Odile's face filled with distress and she backed away as if she were afraid of him, or at least afraid of annoying him. It made him feel good because normally the boot was on the other foot.

'I'll come back another time,' she stammered. 'I don't think your inspector likes me.'

'Oh, I'm sure he does.' To his amazement, Nosjean found he was defending Pel. 'He's not a bad chap really. Underneath, you know. I'm sure he likes you. After all, why not? You're all right.'

She stared at him as if he'd handed her the freedom of the city. 'Do you think so?'

'Of course.'

'Will you be here again?'

'I expect so,' Nosjean said. He was just about to continue that they always gave him the dirty jobs, but he refrained in time and explained instead that it was a job that required a lot of concentration.

'I mustn't stop you working,' she said.

'No. Especially with the Chief about. He's inclined to take a high moral tone about work.'

This time she managed a small sympathetic smile and it seemed to change her face.

'You'd better be careful,' she said.

As Pel had appeared in the drive of 6 Chemin de Champ-Loups, he had been met by Madame Quermel who offered him coffee. She looked attractive and was friendly enough, even if still nervous, and appeared to be working hard at her affability, so that he wondered why none of his own housekeepers ever looked like she did. If Madame Routy had, he thought, he might have done as Darcy had suggested and whipped her into bed, or possibly even married her.

'Mind answering a question or two?' he asked her.

She looked at him nervously then managed to summon up a shaky smile. 'Depends on the question.'

'The night of the murder, a car was seen in the lane. Down near the footbridge. Two people claim to have seen it. I'd like to identify it, because it probably belonged to whoever killed Madame Chenandier. You were out. Did you see it when you returned?'

She gave him a frightened look. 'No, I didn't,' she said quickly. 'I never go down that end of the lane after dark. I simply drove into the drive and left my car in the courtyard. I didn't even look.'

'Sure? Two people saw the car who weren't even looking for it. Didn't you?'

'No.'

Pel shrugged. 'Well, perhaps it had gone by the time you came back,' he said. 'I don't suppose it matters. Probably just a couple necking.'

Finishing his cigarette and draining his coffee cup, he walked down the lane to the small stone bridge that led across the stream, then back on the other side, past the Germain house to Chenandier's and the Layes'. The air, he noticed, was full of the cries of birds and he wondered where they all came from because, normally, French birds were careful to keep out of sight in case they got shot. In the ordinary way, French countrymen fired at everything that moved and he decided the improvement must be due to the ecologists, because young people these days shot with cameras instead of guns.

As he pushed through the long grass, he noticed Odile walking away hurriedly towards the Langres road.

'Wasn't that the Chenandier girl?' he asked as he stopped in front to Nosjean.

Nosjean blushed. 'Yes, Chief.'

'That's the second time I've found her here. She's got her eye on you.'

Nosjean's blush became deeper. 'She only came to talk to me,' he said stiffly.

'Say anything important?'

'No. I think she's just lonely.'

Pel studied Nosjean, giving him full marks for perception. 'You might be right,' he admitted. 'What have you found?'

Nosjean told him, getting worked up a little as he went through the dreary list.

'Calm down,' Pel advised. 'You look as though you're going to burst into flames.'

Nosjean got a grip on himself and, as the release of tension rose like a cloud of steam, he explained about the can of paraffin and the remains of the fire, not mentioning that he'd only examined them because he'd expected Pel to goad him about them.

They walked over to where the fire had been and studied the pasty ashes.

'Checked it?' Pel asked.

'Yes, chief.' Nosjean took out his little plastic bag and indicated the small charred object inside. 'There was this?'

'What is it?'

'Looks like the clip thing off a glove. The press stud that fastens it at the wrist.'

Pel peered at the minute object. 'Anything else?'

Nosjean produced another bag. 'These, Patron.'

'These' were twisted and welded lumps of plastic.

'What do you diagnose them as?'

Nosjean decided to go mad with a decision. 'It looks to me, Chief,' he said, 'as if they're the remains of plastic zip fasteners. You can see what's left of the teeth on this one. Just. The rest have melted away in the fire.'

Pel nodded. 'And that indicates what?' he asked gently.

'Clothing, Patron.'

'What sort?'

'Something with a lot of zips. Anorak. Something like that.'

'Brilliant.' Pel took the plastic bag and peered at the

blackened contents. 'You'll make a detective yet. Anything else?'

'Nothing, Chief. I looked.'

Pel glanced about him. The remains of the fire lay in a small hollow surrounded by willows. 'Would you say this could be seen from the Langres road or the Chemin de Champ-Loups?' he asked.

Nosjean smiled proudly. 'I thought of that, Chief,' he said. 'I checked and it can't. Perhaps the glow, but nothing more.'

'You're doing well. And the paraffin tin?'

Nosjean pointed. 'It was in the willows there. There's a bit of a ditch leading to the stream bed.'

'Within a few yards of the fire. Which indicates?'

'That somebody used the paraffin to burn the clothing that belonged to the zip fasteners.'

Pel stared about him, wondering if Nosjean was right and it *would* have been impossible to see a fire from the road. He came back to the present with a jerk. 'Where's the paraffin can now?' he asked.

Nosjean smiled again. 'I sent it down to the fingerprint boys,' he said. 'I thought there might be something on it.'

'Mon Dieu!' Pel's eyebrows shot up. 'You *are* switched on!'

On his way home, Pel called in the Bar de la Frontière for a glass of white wine. He fended off the proprietor expertly and was sitting outside watching the men playing boules in the dust when Darcq arrived in a battered Peugeot brake with a wooden frame design that had seen better days.

'You always call here?' Pel asked.

Darcq grinned. 'I'm nearly a permanent fixture. Any time now I'll put down roots. They're not bad. They're always good for a drink if I'm short.'

'That your car?'

'Yes.'

'Better not let Traffic see it. It looks to me as if the shock absorbers have gone. The steering looks shot, too. Come to that—' Pel sniffed '—the bodywork isn't much to write home about either.'

'It gets me to and from work.'

'The woodwork's going.'

'Probably woodworm.' Darcq grinned. 'The way the engine turns, you'd think that's got woodworm, too. It's not bad, though. When you turn the wick up, kids on bicycles have a hard time catching me up, believe me.'

Pel was not amused. 'Traffic spend their time looking for cars like that,' he said. 'Inspector Pomereu's very keen on them.'

'Why? Does he collect antiques?' Darcq shrugged. 'Wouldn't help 'em much if they found it,' he said. 'I can't afford to have it repaired. I'm broke again. I'm always broke.'

'You weren't last week,' Pel pointed out. 'You had 3,000 frs.'

Darcq looked at him quickly then he grinned. 'That's right,' he agreed. 'But it's spent now.'

Pel lit a cigarette and pushed the packet across. Darcq helped himself quickly before the offer was withdrawn.

'It belonged to your sister, didn't it?' Pel said.

Darcq's eyebrows shot up but he recovered quickly. 'I won it on a horse,' he insisted. 'I told you.'

'I know you did. But you were lying. You couldn't have won it on a horse. Not that day. The odds were all wrong. We checked.'

'It must have been the day before, then.'

'You're a poor liar, Darcq.'

Darcq gave a wry grin. 'I always was,' he said.

'You took it from your sister's handbag, didn't you?'

Darcq shrugged. 'Yes. How did you know?'

'She'd been to the bank that morning. She drew 3,000 frs. You helped yourself to them.'

'Yes.'

'So you must have been in the house around the time she was murdered.'

Darcq sighed. 'Yes,' he said. 'Just after, I think. Near midnight. I was drunk. I went in. I often went round at

night when Hervé Chenandier was away. That was the only
time I could get in. When he was home, he'd never let me
beyond the front step. I reckoned I could always get
something out of her if I could just get in.'

'How *did* you get in?'

'Through the door. It wasn't locked. Nobody locks their
doors in Aigunay. If I turned up and found it locked, I
assumed she'd gone to bed.'

'And this night?'

'Well, I knew Hervé was away so I turned up in the hope
of using a bit of persuasion.'

'Go by car?'

'Of course.'

'You're lucky Inspector Pomereu didn't catch you if you
were as drunk as you say.'

'I drive well when I'm drunk. Better than when I'm
sober, I sometimes think.'

'Where did you leave your car—Chemin de Champ-
Loups?'

'Not likely. I don't like to be seen going in there. My
sister didn't like me to be seen either. She preferred not to
know me. I left it in Clément-Rémy.'

'How did you know your sister would be awake?'

'I didn't. But then I saw a light in the salon and knew she
was. I even thought I was on to a good thing and that she
might have had a boyfriend in there, because there was a
car in the lane and I knew it didn't belong to any of the
houses there.'

'What sort of car was it?'

'I don't know. I didn't go near it. I thought she might
even be inside it with him. It was just a car. Big. Dark.'

'Where was it?'

'Down near the end of the lane. I knew it didn't belong to
anyone around there. Nobody ever goes down there.'

'Go on.'

'Well, everything was quiet and I finally decided the car
belonged to a courting couple from the city and I went in
the house. I saw her handbag in the hall. It was open, just
dumped on the table by the door. I could see the wad of

money in it, so I helped myself. Because I was drunk, I suppose. Then I wondered if there was anybody about and I looked into the salon. That's when I saw her.'

'Doing what?'

'Doing nothing. She was lying on her back, stark naked except for that thing she had on, staring at the ceiling. It looked like a butcher's shop. I bolted. It sobered me up, I can tell you.'

'Didn't you call anybody? The people you thought were in the car?'

'I was scared stiff and I just headed for the bar here. They were just closing. I stayed for a bit, then I got them to let me have a bottle and I got drunk again.'

'And the money?' Pel said. 'What happened to that?'

'I spent it.' Darcq shuddered. 'Getting drunk. I looked to see if there was blood on it but there wasn't and it all went—that night, and the next. If I'd gone on much longer, I'd have ended up seeing little green men coming through the windows. Seeing her there unnerved me.'

'Why didn't you go to the police?'

'I was scared. I thought they'd think I did it.'

'They did.' Pel shrugged. 'I expect you'll be charged eventually with the theft of the money, which makes two charges with the one for assaulting the police. I'd advise a clean breast. And don't bolt.'

Darcq shook his head. 'Not likely. I'm in enough trouble, as it is.'

Pel wasn't letting up at all. There's jewellery missing, too,' he went on. 'Did you take that?'

Darcq shook his head. 'No. I didn't try. I'd often thought I might, but that night I wouldn't have touched it with a barge pole.'

'You took the money,' Pel pointed out quietly.

'That's different. That was before I found her. And it was there, right in front of my nose. In used notes, too. I knew they'd never trace it. Jewellery's different. They go round the shops.'

'How do you know?'

'Because I once did help myself to a ring. You lot were down on me like a ton of bricks.'

'Do time?'

'No. My sister withdrew the charge and said it was a mistake. She was afraid of getting her name in the paper, I think. Besides, on that night, to get at the jewellery it would have meant going up the stairs and I thought there'd be blood everywhere—perhaps even another stiff. I wouldn't have risked that.'

'You knew where it was then?'

'Yes.'

'Who did take it then?'

Darcq shrugged. 'Whoever did her in, I suppose,' he said.

CHAPTER
FOURTEEN

The following day Nosjean distinguished himself again.

His search round the city jewellers had failed to turn up any of the jewellery but, remembering something one of them had said to him, he had thought perhaps he might push the matter a bit further.

'People from this area who have things to sell,' he'd been told, 'sometimes go to Dôle because they're a bit ashamed of selling family treasures on their own doorsteps in case people recognise them.'

Picking up the telephone and a list of Dôle jewellers, he had sat down for a long session. It had taken him even longer than he'd expected but eventually he turned up what he wanted and, flushed with self-importance and success, he wondered if he might put in a complaint about the number of hours he was being called on to work, and even plucked up courage to put in a call to his girl at her home. She cut him off with a flea in his ear and, wilting like an unwatered hydrangea, he went home, ridden pell-mell by resentment against everybody of higher rank or authority and all girls who considered themselves important.

Darcy was first in the office the next morning and when Pel arrived he was all smiles.

'Enjoy Paris, Patron?' he asked.

'The pavements are harder there even than here.'

Darcy grinned. 'Surely you went out on the town in the evening?'

Pel prided himself on his old-world courtesy, but with Darcy it was inclined to slip a bit at times. Darcy was efficient, keen, ambitious, cheerful, friendly and hard working—all that he should be. At times Pel couldn't stand him.

When Nosjean arrived they listened to his story with interest.

'I've found one of the missing rings. Chief,' he announced. 'In Dôle. Do we take your car or mine?'

Pel's face was blank. 'We take Darcy's,' he said.

'Why Darcy's, Chief?'

Pel ignored the question. 'See Barbièry?' he asked.

'I didn't get the chance, Patron.'

'Then you'll be going to Marsonnay to see *him* in yours, won't you? And if you've any sense, this time you'll enquire first whether he's likely to be home.'

Nosjean disappeared, trying to look dignified and out-raged at the same time. As he passed Darcy, the older sergeant's voice came quietly.

'You didn't expect cries of delight, did you?'

It took them less than an hour to get to Dôle. The road was flat out of the city but as they headed south-west it began to rise. As they came to Dôle, they could see the forest of Chaux on a vine-clad slope, then they were driving between the old Spanish Renaissance-style houses. Pel had sat quietly as Darcy drove. Now he came suddenly to life, lit a cigarette, filled the car with smoke, and sat up abruptly.

'If you were going to murder someone, Darcy,' he said, 'how would you do it?'

Darcy shrugged. 'I expect I'd use a two-two rifle.'

Pel stared at him. 'Why not a revolver?'

Darcy grinned. 'French game laws being what they are, you don't have to have a licence for a two-two and you do for a revolver. So, with a two-two, it's quite legal.'

Pel stared at him, irritated by his levity. 'The trouble with you, Darcy,' he said, 'is that you don't take your job seriously enough.'

Darcy shrugged. 'I can tell a liar,' he pointed out. 'And, as far as I can make out, everybody in this business is one. They're all involved one way or another.'

Pel frowned. 'Laye with Madame Chenandier. Chenandier with Madame Quermel.'

'Fornication Corner,' Darcy said.

Pel nodded. 'And Darcq hanging round all the time for everything he could get. Somebody was in that house that night and I want to know who. Laye didn't see him. Darcq didn't. The gardener didn't. And neither did the two women who were in the house, or Chenandier because he was in Paris. Neither, come to that, did the neighbours. So who was it?' Pel gestured angrily. 'Sit on Darcq. Get him in again and give him a going-over. See if you can break his story.'

There was a long silence then Pel spoke again. 'When you checked Chenandier's clothes,' he asked, 'did you see any anoraks?'

'No. Quermel said he never wore them.'

'She volunteered the information?'

'Not really. I was checking everything that I thought he might have been wearing that night in the rain—waterproofs, that sort of thing. His daughter said he usually wore a plastic mackintosh—the one he gave us that was in his suitcase. I asked about anything else he might have had. After all, it was raining hard, you remember, and I suggested anoraks myself. But Quermel said he detested them because they reminded him too much of the jump jacket he wore in the paras. Why, Chief?'

Pel rubbed his nose thoughtfully. 'Because Nosjean found a zip fastener in the remains of that fire,' he said.

'And I noticed that Laye wears anoraks. There was one in his car. A new-looking one covered with zips.'

The shop in Dôle was small and dark, and the old man and the girl who occupied it seemed dwarfed by the single brilliant light that threw its beam down on to the counter. The jeweller placed the ring on a piece of red baize.

'Not very valuable, Monsieur,' he asked.

Pel's eyebrows rose. 'What is it?' he asked.

'A zirkon. It's a good zirkon, of course, but zirkons don't compare with rubies, sapphires, emeralds or diamonds. It's the sort of ring a woman might wear during the day when she's pottering about the house. When she wished to be elegant, she'd wear something more valuable.'

It occurred to Pel that if *he'd* been married, on the pay he got such a ring would probably be his wife's pride and joy, because she'd have had no other.

'Who brought it in?' he asked. 'A woman?'

'No, Monsieur. A man.'

'Describe him.'

'Tallish. Dark.'

'Working-class type?'

'Yes. I thought he was wearing his best suit for the occasion.'

'Didn't you suspect he might have stolen it?'

The jeweller smiled. 'You'd be surprised at the type of people who come in these days to sell jewellery. Most of it's quite straightforward. He said it was his mother's and that after the war his family had lost their money. He'd had to take a job in a factory and they were having to get rid of things to make ends meet.'

Darcy frowned and glanced at Pel. 'Sounds like Darcq, Chief,' he said. 'He works at FMPS.'

The jeweller looked up. 'I don't think *this* one worked in a factory, Monsieur,' he said. 'Or even in a garage. Despite what he said. He hadn't a factory worker's hands. We get them in sometimes, buying things for their wives. Some of them have a lot of money these days and they think jewellery is a good investment. They usually have longish nails—so they can pick up things like screws—and usually there's dirt under them. They aren't dirty men, you understand, but it's impossible to get rid of all the grease.'

'And this man's nails?' Pel asked.

'No oil. His nails were short and broken and cracked, as though he worked with something rougher than tools.'

'Such as what?'

'Stone, Monsieur. Or soil. His hands were hard and scarred with work. But the work wasn't work that contained oil or grease.'

'A gardener's hands?' Pel asked.

The jeweller smiled. 'You have one such on your list?'

Back at the office, Nosjean couldn't contain himself.

'We've found the murder weapon,' he said.

'Who has?' Darcy said.

'Those chaps I organised.'

'The way you're going on,' Darcy said, 'you'll make yourself ill.'

Nosjean frowned. The only thing that was likely to make him ill, he felt, was frustration caused by his inability to get to closer quarters with his girl friend. 'They were ploughing about any old how,' he said. 'I got them doing it properly. I got them on a square search.'

'What's a square search?'

'It's the way rescue ships search the sea.'

'You brought in rescue ships?'

Pel interrupted before Nosjean went into his orphan-of-the-storm act. 'Where is it now?' he asked.

'Leguyader's got it. It's being dusted down for fingerprints.'

Leguyader had the poker on a bench. It was rusting a little from the dew on its steel surface. 'Someone made an attempt to clean it with grass,' he said. 'But there are still traces of blood and hair on it. *Her* blood and *her* hair.'

Pel bent over it. 'Anything else it can tell us?'

'What more do you want? Parma violets? That's what was used to kill her.'

'Any fingerprints?'

'Plenty. Chenandier's, Odile Chenandier's, Madame Quermel's, Madame Chenandier's, that brother of hers—even the gardener's. *He* probably touched it when he brought in logs for the fire.'

Pel sniffed. 'He might have touched it when he used it to hammer her head flat, too,' he observed. 'Anything else?'

'A smudge or two which were probably caused by a glove or might also have been caused by someone doing the cleaning and picking it up with a duster in the hand. That's how people cleaning often do pick up things like this.'

'You know, of course?'

Leguyader smiled smugly. 'Do it for my wife sometimes,' he said.

He tossed a sheet of paper across. 'Report on Laye's clothes,' he said. 'Nothing. Madame Chenandier's hairs. That's all. But if they were in the habit of going into clinches occasionally, that's not unusual and certainly doesn't prove he did her in.'

Pel stared at the paper bitterly, then he picked it up and turned to Darcy. 'Let's go and see the gardener,' he said.

In the car Pel was silent. Before long, he was going to have to admit to Brisard that he had no firm suspect. There were one or two he might have brought in, but he knew perfectly well he could never make a charge of murder stick. He might throw the gardener in front of the judge for being in possession of Madame Chenandier's ring, or Darcq for having her money, but while he knew that would please Brisard, he preferred to wait quietly. Sooner or later someone would make a false move. There weren't many after all now, because eliminating the Germains had reduced the field a bit. So who would it be? Laye? Madame Quermel? Odile Chenandier? Chenandier himself? None of them could give any definite proof of where they were at the time of the murder.

It was midday when they stopped the car in the Chemin de Champ-Loups. Pel walked down the drive and round the back of the house to the garden. The gardener had propped a spade against the side of the stone-built shed and on the bench they could see a bottle of wine and the plastic box that contained his lunch. Albertini was eating but as he saw Pel, he jumped to his feet and wiped his hands on his shirt.

Pel gestured. 'Sit down,' he said.

The Italian sat down again on the backless chair. He was clearly nervous and kept wiping his hands on his shirt, his dark-skinned face backgrounded by the whitewashed wall with its scrawled reminders, addresses and telephone numbers.

Pel produced the ring the jeweller had found. 'Recognise this?' he asked.

The gardener's face fell. 'Si, Signore,' he said quietly.

'Was it you who sold it?'

'Yes.'

'Where are the others?'

The Italian's head jerked up. 'What others, Signore?'

'The other things that are missing?'

'I do not know anything else is missing, Signore.'

Pel glanced at Darcy. 'When did you sell this?' he asked.

'The day after the murder, Signore.'

'Where did you get it?'

'Here in the garden. She took it off. She is doing something and the ring is so big it keeps catching. She put it down on the steps there and forgot it. It is still there two days later. She does not even miss it. So I take it and keep it. I was going to wait in case she make a fuss about it and, if she does, say I'd found it. I think there might be a reward. But she never does. I never even hear her mention it. It couldn't have been much to her. So I decide I will sell it when everything is quiet, but then she is killed and I think I must get rid of it. I go to Dôle on the motorbike.'

'Pity you didn't realise that all jewellers are notified about missing jewellery,' Darcy commented.

The Italian gestured with his hands earnestly. 'I don't know about any missing jewellery,' he insisted. 'I never even went in the house except to take in logs or perhaps to telephone. She didn't like me going in the house.'

Who didn't?'

'Madame. She once sees me in there and calls me a dirty

Italian. Only the housekeeper ever treat me properly.'

'Get on well with her?' Darcy said.

'Yes. She is kind. I tell her my troubles.'

'You got some?'

'People think I am stupid because I don't speak the language so well. They also consider I'm a criminal because I'm a gardener and Italian.'

Pel thought for a while. 'The night of the murder,' he said. 'When you came away from the house you went to your sister's at Boux. Which way did you go?'

'Down the lane, Signore.'

'The lane doesn't lead anywhere. It becomes a footpath. Nobody goes down there.'

'*I* do. All the time. You can take a motorbike down there. It's a bit bumpy but it saves going all the way round. It leads on to the Langres road, then I turn off for Bazay or Boux.'

'Did you see a car down there?'

The Italian's eyes flickered. 'No, Signore, I didn't.'

'Three other people who *didn't* go down the lane saw it. But you who *did* go down the lane missed it.'

The Italian shrugged. 'It is dark, Signore. Very dark. Perhaps I am not thinking about it. It's bumpy down there and narrow, and you have to concentrate. If you don't, the bike goes into the stream.'

Pel gestured at the Italian. 'Get someone to whip him down to Leguyader,' he said to Darcy. 'I want a check on his clothes for blood.'

'Leguyader's going to be pleased.'

'Can't be helped. In the meantime, let's see who else's about.'

Madame Quermel was shopping and only Odile Chenandier was in the house.

'She'll do, I suppose,' Pel said gloomily. 'You can ask her about that teacher she attacked.'

Odile Chenandier received them unwillingly in her flat. It was decorated in a modern style, with black and purple walls, comfortless furniture and blown-up pictures of pop stars. She was dressed in tattered jeans and a singlet that showed her breasts. She was nervous with them and made no attempt to offer them a cigarette or a drink or even a seat.

'I'd like to check round the house,' Pel said.

She eyed them worriedly. 'I don't know if I should—'

'I could look myself,' Pel pointed out.

Her hand fluttered. 'I meant, I wondered if he'd want me to.'

In the end she allowed herself to be persuaded and Pel went carefully through the house checking cupboards and drawers. She seemed pleased that he appeared to find nothing that might incriminate anyone, but when Pel tossed at her the discovery they'd made about her attack on a mistress at school, her eyes widened and grew hot with anger.

'Yes,' she admitted. 'I did hit her. She'd been picking on me. Because I couldn't cook. She said all Frenchwomen could cook, but there are as many bad cooks in France as anywhere else. I don't even *like* cooking.'

'She provoked you?'

'She had been doing ever since I went there.'

'The psychiatrist said you were hysterical.'

The sallow skin flushed. 'I was nothing of the sort. I was angry.'

Pel's feet ached and he pulled a chair forward. 'Did you hit your mother with the poker?'

'No.'

'You sure?'

'Of course I'm sure. How could I?'

Pel didn't mention that he'd come across less likely murderers. 'Did you ever hit her with *anything*?' he asked.

'Yes. My hand.'

'You slapped her?'

'No.' Tears welled up and her head turned in her desperate anguished way. 'I used my fist.'

'Your fist?' Pel glanced at Darcy.

The girl caught the look and hurried on in an attempt to explain. 'I was so angry. She'd been sneering at me, asking why I never brought boys home. But she never encouraged me! She never helped me! After I hit her, she tried to be pleasant.' Odile paused and sighed. 'But not much.'

Pel sat quietly, thinking, and she lit a small cigar. She didn't appear to enjoy it much and he guessed it was part of her attempts to appear sophisticated and in charge of herself.

'Why did you go to your mother's room after you found her dead?' he asked, and she gave him a terror-stricken look.

'You did go, didn't you?'

'No.'

'Then why were there traces of blood on the stairs and by the drawer where her jewellery was kept? There was blood on your shoe. You'd picked it up when you found her.'

Odile said nothing, her face grey with fear.

'All this is correct, isn't it?'

She spoke at last. 'Yes.'

'Did *you* take the jewellery?'

There was a long silence then she nodded. 'I didn't know there was blood on my shoe. There couldn't have been much because I looked on the stair carpet and I couldn't see any.'

'There *wasn't* much,' Pel agreed. 'But there was enough. Did your father know you had the jewels?'

'He guessed. He knew I'd always loved them.'

'Why didn't he tell us?'

Odile's shoulders moved heavily. 'He threatened to, so I threatened to tell you about him and Madame Quermel.'

'So you knew about them?'

She nodded dumbly.

'What about your mother? Did you know she had a lover?'

Odile sat in silence for a while then she nodded again.

'Did you know it was Monsieur Laye from next door.'

'How did you find out?'

'Laye's daughter told us.'

She was silent again, for so long Pel thought she'd forgotten them, then she sighed and straightened her shoulders. 'I wish I'd known she knew,' she said.

'Why?'

'It would have been someone to talk to, someone to share something with.'

Pel studied her. 'You didn't really love your parents, did you?' he asked.

She looked up at him, agony in her eyes, then she shook her head. 'They never allowed me to,' she whispered.

'And the jewels? Where are they now?'

'I deposited them in my bank. As an unidentified parcel. I said they were a few things belonging to me and I was depositing them because I was frightened after the murder.'

Pel turned away. 'Go along with her and collect them, Darcy,' he said wearily.

CHAPTER
FIFTEEN

While Pel and Darcy had gone to Dôle, Nosjean had gone sullenly to Marsonnay to see Barbièry. It was a long way and Marsonnay was a hot ugly little town that depressed Nosjean even more than he was normally depressed.

Barbièry was an enormous lantern-jawed man with hands like coal grabs and a set of teeth that were palpably false and moved in his mouth as he talked. He had a curious manner that worried Nosjean and he decided that Barbièry probably wasn't quite right in the head. Judging by the shelves full of railway timetables and the experience of his own little search through them, Nosjean came to the conclusion that anyone who could find a railway timetable entertaining *had* to have something wrong with him.

'Well, you might get via Montluçon and Bourges,' Barbièry was saying. 'But I doubt if you'd get there quicker than by going direct. And if you went via Nancy it would take hours longer. Do you know, Monsieur—' Barbièry gestured '—in England it takes all of four hours to go from

London to Sheffield and all night to go to Aberdeen. Yet those British have the nerve to sneer at French trains. There are always too many people in this world inclined to run our railways down. Even Giulle.'

'But Giulle was a railwayman himself,' Nosjean pointed out.

'Yes.' Barbièry seemed to have forgotten Giulle again and was lost once more in the intricacies of railway travel as he stared at his timetables. He sighed, and went on. 'I always thought it a pity when they electrified,' he said. 'Of course, it's more efficient these days and the direct current motor with its excellent accelerating characteristics, light weight and simple speed control is ideal for the purpose. But we lost something when we lost steam engines.' He glanced at his timetables again. 'He might have gone via Langres, Chaumont and Châlons,' he said. 'But it wouldn't ever be quicker because the line from Basle and Belfort joins at Langres and there's always a hold-up for the Swiss passengers, and at Châlons they join from Metz, Saarbrucken and the rest of Germany.'

They seemed to be getting nowhere and as Nosjean fidgeted impatiently, Barbièry's pale eyes gleamed. 'He was a traitor to the railways, Monsieur,' he said.

'Who was?'

'Giulle, of course. He took money from them but he was always running them down.'

'Wanders a bit,' Pel had said. Nosjean decided that Barbièry wandered *a lot*. 'Yes,' he agreed. 'About the trains—'

'Of course.' Barbièry smiled. 'He could have gone south, of course, and picked up the Riviera Express at Nevers, but that would take time.' He gestured. 'Do you know, in 1955, the USA had a greater railway mileage than any other country in the world. Two hundred and twenty-one thousand miles, they had. For her size, though, France always led the way in innovation. The war did untold damage to French railways—all that bombing—and they've never been the same since. But he never allowed for that, did he?'

'Who?'

'Giulle. He was constantly running them down.'

'Well, we all do that a bit with our jobs,' Nosjean said. 'Even me with the police.'

'Not like *him*, Monsieur.' Barbièry's eyes widened and Nosjean decided finally that he was going to get nothing because Barbièry was clearly potty. 'I never spoke to him on a single occasion when he didn't run them down. And, you know, I could have sent him from Paris to Toulouse, going by night, quicker than he could go from Cologne to Munich.'

It didn't make sense to Nosjean. One minute, Barbièry appeared to be perfectly normal and helpful, the next as crazy as they came.

'Is that so?' he said.

'When he just went on and on, it got too much for me.'

'I can imagine,' Nosjean said.

'So I let him have it.'

'Have what?'

'It's a figure of speech, Monsieur,' Barbièry said. 'The gun.'

'What gun?'

'*His* gun. He was always out with it. He said he shot a Nazi with it during the war but I don't believe him. He wasn't old enough. He was just a big talker. He wasn't as old as me and I wasn't old enough for that.'

Nosjean listened to the babbling for a moment then it suddenly dawned on him what he'd heard.

'You let him have it,' he repeated. 'With the gun.'

'That's right, Monsieur.'

'*His* gun? The one that killed him?'

'That's right. If ever a man asked for it, he did.'

'He asked for—' Nosjean gulped and he gripped his notebook tighter. 'You mean *you* shot him?'

'Why not?'

Nosjean slowly began to put away his notebook and pencil, with a feeling that he might need both hands free. Carefully, he eased his handcuffs in his pocket and moved warily in his chair.

Barbièry was staring at him now, prattling on about the route from Dijon to Bordeaux. Nosjean stopped him with difficulty. He put aside the book and looked up with a crazy smile.

'Let's get this straight,' Nosjean said.

He shifted uneasily. They'd been trying to find out who'd killed Giulle for weeks now. They'd asked about the women he knew, the people he owed money to, anybody who might have upset him at work, all the usual stuff they went through every time someone was found with his head blown off, his throat cut or with a knife stuck in his back. *For weeks*! And here was this madman claiming he'd done it! His next-door neighbour!

'Let's get this straight,' Nosjean said again. 'You say you *killed* him.'

'Yes. Of course.'

'Why?' This was important. There were always lunatics offering themselves for every murder that occurred. Most of them were suffering from a need for the limelight, and confessions of that sort didn't mean much. 'Why?' he repeated.

Barbièry was staring at Nosjean as though puzzled at his dimness. 'Because we've lived next door to each other,' he explained. 'All our lives. I'd had enough of him. So I shot him.'

'Because you'd had enough of him?'

'Yes.'

'Is that all?'

'It's sufficient, isn't it?'

'Why are you telling me this now?' Nosjean asked. 'You've not mentioned it before to anyone.'

Barbièry shrugged. 'I think it's gone on long enough,' he said.

For a while Nosjean tried to assimilate what had happened. It seemed to be the most incredible luck. But then he realised there was more to it than that. A confession wasn't sufficient. He now had to get Barbièry to a police station and, by the look in his eye and the size of him, it wasn't going to be easy.

He cleared his throat. 'I think you'd better come with me, Monsieur,' he said. 'I think we ought to have a statement from you.'

Barbièry looked startled and clutched the heavy time-table he'd been using to his chest. 'What about?'

'About killing Giulle.'

'Is that all?' Barbièry's stare became suddenly cunning and hostile. 'I'm not coming to your office just for that.'

Nosjean stood up. 'I'm afraid you'll have to, Monsieur,' he said firmly.

He wasn't expecting what happened next because he'd never thought of a railway timetable as an offensive weapon. When it hit him in the face he realised just how offensive it could be. Since it consisted of a kilo and a half of tightly packed paper, it knocked him half silly. Fortunately, it wasn't hard, but it threw him off balance, so that he fell over a stool and landed on the floor. Rolling sideways, he saw Barbièry about to kick him in the face with his great boot so, in desperation, he grabbed his ankle and yanked. As Barbièry went over, so did the table with Barbièry's reference books and the glasses from which they'd been drinking, and Barbièry's head cracked smartly against the wall. While he was still dizzy, Nosjean clapped the hand-cuffs on.

It was obviously still more than he could manage to handle the giant on his own, so he dived for the exit and slamming the door, clutched the handle and yelled to a waiter standing in the entrance to a bar across the street, to telephone for the police.

The waiter seemed a little slow. 'What for?' he asked.

'He's gone berserk!'

'Why?'

'Never mind why?' Nosjean screamed. 'Do it! And quick!'

'Why? Who're you?'

Nosjean had a bright idea. 'Look,' he said. 'If you don't, he'll be out of here soon and if he gets out, I'll take refuge over there and then it'll be your bar that'll get smashed up.'

It was unorthodox but it was enough to start the waiter moving.

During the afternoon, Pel sent a car to the FPMS factory and picked up Darcq. Darcy spent the whole afternoon vainly pecking at him, arguing, shouting, sometimes using a quiet sibilance full of threats. For an hour, Pel relieved him, but he found he was getting nowhere, too, and he wasn't sorry when Darcy returned and took over once more.

Somehow he had a feeling that they'd reached the crunch. The solution to the case was just out of reach somewhere in the shadows and they just couldn't stretch out and touch it.

As he lifted his hand to take his hat from its peg, Brisard rang for him and asked him to call in his room in the Palais de Justice. Pel sighed and set off through the old narrow streets with their tall flat-fronted buildings and silent courts. The heat was still intense and the narrow alleys he chose seemed to be airless. The Palais de Justice seemed to belong to another world, with its ancient halls, cool, stained glass and carved woodwork. Pel decided it was far too good for someone like Brisard.

The judge had obviously had a session with the Procureur and had decided to be difficult. Pel fended him off half-heartedly. He was uneasy. Everybody seemed to have wandered into or around the Chenandier house within minutes of each other without being seen—the gardener, Darcq, Madame Quermel, Laye, Odile; perhaps, somehow, even Chenandier himself. The minutes that separated them seemed important.

'Give me twenty-four hours,' he begged. 'That's all. Twenty-four hours.'

He walked back to his own office, deep in thought and worried. As he was about to leave a second time, Nosjean burst in. He had a black eye and a livid bruise on his jaw. To Pel's surprise he was grinning, and seemed to be hovering above the floor like a humming bird in his excitement. He was clearly hypnotised with visions of glory.

'What happened to you?' Pel demanded. 'You have the self-satisfaction of a major prophet once again proved right by the Almighty.'

Nosjean's grin widened. 'I've found your murderer, Chief,' he chirruped.

'Which murderer?'

'The railwayman. Giulle. I got it while I was checking the trains. It was Barbièry. He came out with it just like that, while we were talking about timetables. He said *he* did it.'

Pel sniffed. 'Confessions don't count for much with a good lawyer. They've got to be sound.'

'This one *is*. No lawyer would bother to try to get round this one.'

'Why not?'

'Because it's so stupid it can't be anything else but true. Nobody could have thought up anything as silly as this. He attacked me and I had to arrest him. The doctor I got to look at him at Marsonnay said his family have a history of instability and his father was put away, it seems, for half-killing a grocer.'

Nosjean seemed delighted with himself but he was wise enough not to suggest that anyone had been neglectful. 'Mind,' he said, 'it was something that wasn't exactly shouted about, Patron. There was no reason to suspect him until he started claiming to have done it.'

Pel nodded. 'What about the trains?' he asked.

Nosjean's jaw dropped. ''Trains, Patron?'

'You went to ask about train times.'

'I didn't get around to that one, Patron.'

Pel sniffed. 'You're falling down on the job,' he said. He waved away Nosjean's indignant protest. 'Better inform the Procureur,' he advised. 'And for God's sake, go and catch Judge Brisard before he goes home. Make as much of it as you can. It'll keep him off my neck.'

'Then can I go home, Patron? I'm due for a night off.'

'Your girl getting worried?'

'I know *I* am.'

As Pel nodded, Nosjean galloped away, dropping pencils and notebook on his desk as he went. Pel watched him,

DEATH SET TO MUSIC

wondering why he had never felt like that in his life and whether he'd missed something on the way somewhere.

As he drove home, Pel decided his stomach was playing him up again. Convinced he had an ulcer coming on, he worked a couple of bismuth tablets out of the box one-handed and popped them in his mouth. With Madame Routy's assistance, the evening was going to be murder.

When he arrived, she was watching television with the volume control turned up as far as it would go and the house was shuddering under the shock. He could hear the noise even as he drove up the street. Didier Darras was sitting on the front steps waiting for him, reading a book, his fishing-rod on the path beside him.

Neither of them spoke and, as Pel appeared, he picked up the rod, pushed it through the open window of the car, and climbed in alongside Pel. Pel shrugged, and drove to the nearest bar.

'Coca Cola or Pschitt?' he asked.

Didier grinned. 'Pschitt. Coca Cola's American.'

'Patriot, eh?'

'They're taking over everywhere.'

'I don't think they'll take you over.'

They finished their drinks without saying much and headed for the river.

Pel had brought two bottles of beer with him and a ham sandwich he'd bought at the bar, and he sat and ate and drank quietly while the boy threw out his line.

'Biting?' he asked.

'No. But it doesn't matter. I don't come to catch fish.'

Pel's eyebrows rose. 'Why do you come then?'

'I like sitting here. If I catch a fish it's something extra.'

'Philosopher as well as a patriot, eh? Doubtless you'll take a different view when you're older and consider some things worth putting yourself out for.'

'What things?'

'Girls.'

The line sagged and the boy tugged at it.

'Bite?'

'No. Reeds.'

Pel sat up. The line ended among a tuft of green surrounded by swirling water. 'You'll never get it out of there,'
he said.

Didier was unperturbed. 'I can always go in and get it.'

'It must be a good metre deep just there.'

'Won't matter.'

'You can't get out there, mon brave, without getting wet
through and your clothes covered with mud.'

The boy was dragging his shirt over his head. 'I can
always take 'em off,' he said.

Madame Routy regarded them icily when they returned. 'I
never know when you're in for a meal or out these days,'
she said. 'It'll have to be cold. I can't keep things hot for
ever.'

Pel seemed thoughtful, and didn't even respond when
she switched on the television. Instead, he was just hurrying to the garden when the telephone went.

It was Darcy. He sounded tired.

'Judge Brisard's been on the phone, Chief,' he said.
'He's tickled pink about Nosjean picking up Barbièry.'

'Well, it'll do Nosjean's ego a bit of good,' Pel admitted.
'Get anything from Darcq?'

'He sticks to the story, Chief. He's a congenital liar and
he finds it hard to remember what he said last time. But he's
also frightened and that's making him careful. His story's
tight. Do I let him go?'

'You'll have to.'

'Right. By the way, Leguyader announces negative re-
sults from the Italian's clothes. He's just rung up.'

Pel frowned and Darcy called out. 'You still there,
Patron?'

'Yes. Have you got something else?'

'I think we might have had a break. The fingerprint boys
rang. That paraffin can Nosjean found. It's got Quermel's
prints on it. So has that brandy bottle he found.'

'Does Quermel drink brandy?'

'Not so you'd notice, Patron. And, anyway, even if

swigging out of the bottle was something women like her normally did, she'd hardly be likely to sit there in the field slugging back that amount, unless she had a good reason.'

'Such as what?'

'Trying to work up Dutch courage to do something that required an effort. Do we go and see her?'

'How do you feel?'

'Tired, Patron.'

'How about the others?'

'Misset's with his wife and new baby. Krauss set off for Dôle to see that jeweller and he's not back yet. Lagé was put on some job of the Procureur's again. And some fool gave Nosjean the night off.'

Feeling a coward, Pel said nothing and Darcy went on. 'It'll have to be the Old Guard, Patron,' he said. 'You and me.'

'Right,' Pel agreed. 'But let's leave it until later in the evening. Get a meal then call round and fetch me. We'll see her when we feel rested and she feels tired. She might be more inclined to talk then, and we might do better.'

While Pel was talking on the telephone to Darcy, a Madame Valentine Chornay, of Rue Achille-Luchaire, Bazay, was just wiping her hands to put a newly-prepared rabbit pie in the oven. It was for her husband and, though he invariably arrived home late from the bar where he went for his apéritif, he was also usually hungry and in a bad temper if his food wasn't just so.

Her husband's casual attitude to time created endless problems for Madame Chornay so, to be on the safe side, she always took the greatest possible care. Wiping the flour from her hands, she stood back from the table to admire the pastry flowers on the crust she'd made, slapped the fingers of one of the children who was reaching out to stuff a piece of pastry into its mouth, and lifted the dish. She was just on the point of turning from the table to the oven when there was the sound of a revving engine and a crash from the road outside. It was a metallic crash and was followed by tinkling glass and a screeching sound as if something steel was being dragged along the road. With it there was a cry of anguish and terror and again the revving engine and she knew exactly what had happened.

Accidents had occurred before outside her house, which was on a corner, and she'd more than once ministered to some shocked and bleeding motorist; so, without panic, she put the dish down, carefully—because her husband would still come home for his meal, accident or no accident— adjured the children not to touch it, and hurried outside.

It was just growing dark and the village was deserted; there was no sign of a car and, looking up and down the road, she wondered if she'd been mistaken. Then she saw the marks on the tarmacadam where something had scraped the surface, and the torn turf opposite. Heading across the road, she saw a red-painted motobicyclette like the one her husband rode to work lying in the ditch and then, underneath it, legs and a protruding hand.

With a gasp, she jumped into the ditch and tried to pull the motorbicycle free but it was too heavy for her and she began to scream for help. One of her children appeared in the doorway of the house and she gestured towards the lights of the bar in the village.

'Go and fetch Pappy,' she yelled. 'I need help. There's been an accident.'

As the child bolted up the street, she turned her attention once more to the man underneath the motorbicycle. There seemed to be a great deal of torn flesh and she noticed that he was bleeding from the nose and ears, something she'd learned over the years to regard as serious. Then she realised she recognised the machine and it dawned on her she also knew the man underneath.

Since Madame Routy had no intention for this evening at least of giving way over the television, as Pel waited for Darcy, he and Didier played Scrabble in the kitchen. Inevitably, Pel lost heavily.

'You're not very good,' Didier said.

'I'm not very clever really,' Pel pointed out.

Before they could start another game, Darcy telephoned. 'We're not going to see Quermel, Chief,' he said.

'Why not?' Pel's eyebrows shot up. 'Something happened to her?'

'No, Patron. It's the gardener, Albertini. He's been found with his motorbike in a ditch near his lodgings at Bazay.'

'Murdered?'

'No. Hit and run. It's just come in. Pomereu, of Traffic, passed it on and the duty dogsbody took it.'

Without a second thought, Pel knew it was connected with the Chenandier case. The coincidence was just too strong to be otherwise.

'I'll be down,' he said. 'Ring Krauss and Misset. Leave messages that they're to ring in. We'll probably need them. And it looks like Nosjean's going to lose his night off again.'

Darcy gave a tired sigh. 'He's lost it, Patron. I've already called him in to sit on the telephone. He should be here any time now. He didn't sound very pleased. He was at his girlfriend's.'

By the time Pel arrived at headquarters Nosjean had worked himself into a bitter mood. He seemed to have been on duty for ever. He'd been reaping clouds of glory by arresting somebody dangerous but now all he was doing was sitting on the end of the telephone. Somebody had to do it, of course, but nobody enjoyed the duty and it was usually given to the newest recruit—Nosjean.

He sat in the sergeants' room and didn't very much like what he saw. It wasn't even a room. In fact, it was just one corner of the main office and, with its green-painted walls, grey doors, iron staircase and windows that looked out on to the Paris-Lyon railway line, it had the charm and comfort of the inside of a tank. He was laying his reports in front of Darcy as Pel headed for his office. 'There's a girl been attacked near the Place Clemenceau and somebody stabbed a lorry driver in a bar just off the N17. Both cases are being handled by the uniformed branch. There's also a kid who robbed a supermarket at Talant. Lagé's handling him. He's just got back.' Nosjean waved vaguely and Darcy saw the other detective leaning over a dim-looking youngster in a red track-suit with 'Toulouse' in large white letters on the back.

'That the lot?' Darcy asked.

Nosjean frowned. 'Apart from an English tourist who says he's been robbed. Krauss's got him.'

'Where was it?' Darcy asked.

'The Paradiso. That's that brothel near the Ateliers SNCF. What was he doing there?'

Darcy grinned tiredly. 'What do you think he was doing? Or haven't you got around to that yet?'

Nosjean blushed. 'I meant what was an *Englishman* doing there.'

'Same as the Frenchmen, I expect.'

'No, no!' Nosjean was growing angry. 'I mean it's not the sort of place to find an Englishman.'

'Why not, for God's sake? They're made the same as us.'

'I mean it's down in the industrial zone. How did he get there?'

In fact, it hadn't been difficult. The Englishman had met a Frenchman in a bar who'd encouraged him to go along with him. The Englishman had been hoping for a bit of fun—after all, that's what the French got up to all the time, wasn't it?—but, not understanding the language very well, he'd found himself instead in a third-rate brothel and had promptly been relieved of his wallet containing his French money, his English money, his traveller's cheques, his passport, his bank card, the photo of his mother, his library ticket, his driving licence, his AA card and a letter from a travel agency indicating a booking for a hotel in Nice.

Krauss was questioning him in the corner away from the traffic, and he'd obviously decided that the Englishman was a fool. The city didn't boast much in the way of brothels—it wasn't Paris or Marseilles—but it had one or two unofficial ones and anybody who went poking his nose into them when he couldn't even speak the language properly *had* to be a fool.

'J'ai perdé—perdi—perdu—' Krauss waited for him to make up his mind '—mon bourse.'

'Bourse?'

'Yes. I mean, oui. Bourse. Purse. Wallet. Wall-it.'

Nosjean sighed and looked hopefully at Darcy. 'When will I get a relief?' he asked.

'Not tonight, old son. There's nobody to spare.'

'What about Misset?'

'His wife's just had her baby. I expect he's holding her hand and looking at it like a mare with glanders. You'll just have to hang on.'

As Pel reappeared from his office, his pockets jammed with notebooks, pens, pencils—and spare cigarettes in case he went mad and smoked the two packets he'd been carrying when he'd arrived—he stopped and listened to Krauss questioning the boy in the red track-suit who had robbed the supermarket.

'I got the stuff into the Deux Chevaux through the back door,' the boy was saying.

'Through the back door,' Krauss repeated.

'I thought I could sell it at a profit.'

'Well, since you hadn't paid for it,' Pel observed dryly, 'it would be a profit, wouldn't it?'

As the boy looked up at him, he gestured at the track-suit. 'Do you play for Toulouse?'

'No. But I'm a keen supporter.'

Pel studied the track-suit thoughtfully, then he nodded and vanished. As he passed Nosjean, the young detective gave him a bitter look. Darcy patted Nosjean's shoulder sympathetically and followed him out. At the door he turned and indicated the telephone. 'Don't let it get away, mon brave,' he said.

When they reached Bazay, Traffic was already handling the case and the village seemed to be full of dark blue vans. An ambulance was just disappearing towards the city.

Pel stared at the bent motobicyclette at the side of the road, the broken glass and the small patch of blood on the grass.

'Dead?' he asked.

'No.' Inspector Pomereu of Traffic gestured. 'But I expect he will be soon. Either way, he's going to be in hospital for a long time. He's got a fractured skull and multiple injuries. I doubt if he'll ever properly recover.'

'No idea how it happened?'

'None. Our chap in the village was on the spot within minutes. There was no sign of the car. The woman opposite—' the inspector gestured at Madame Chornay standing in the middle of a group of policemen across the road, watched by her neighbours '—she heard the crash. She was cooking at the time and she wiped her hands and ran out. It took her only a matter of seconds. He was lying in the ditch with the bike on top of him.'

'Did you take photographs?'

Inspector Pomereu was a thin sallow man with a sharp alert expression. He had a reputation for missing nothing and he answered Pel tartly.

'Of course.'

'I shall want copies,' Pel said.

Pomereu's eyebrows shot up. 'Of a traffic case?'

'Yes.'

'It might have been a genuine accident.'

'And it might not.'

Pomereu studied Pel. 'Do you know him?'

'Unfortunately, yes.'

'Suspect in something you're handling?'

'Yes.'

'Well, you'll not get much out of him for some time—if ever.'

Pel shrugged. 'We'd better have somebody by his bed just in case,' he said. 'What about the car? No indication what it was?'

'None. Nobody saw it. And apart from the bang, nobody heard it. There was no sign of it and there were no tyre marks.'

'No signs of sudden braking?'

'No.'

'As if he simply saw him, and hit him without slowing down?'

'It was dark.'

Pel nodded. 'I wasn't thinking of that,' he said.

CHAPTER
SIXTEEN

When Pel arrived at headquarters the next day, it was late. There was a note to say that Albertini had died during the night and there were copies of Inspector Pomereu's pictures from the photographic department awaiting him. Pel read the note that accompanied them, then took the packet of pictures, opened it, studied the contents, sighed and lit a cigarette.

In the sergeants' room, Nosjean was back on the telephone. Misset had just arrived and Nosjean was clearly buttering him up in the hope of being able to hand over the duty.

'How's the baby?' he was asking.

Misset beamed. 'Fine,' he said.

'And the wife?'

'Also fine.'

'You on duty?'

'No.'

'Oh!' Nosjean's bright friendly expression vanished and Misset grinned.

'Why?' he asked. 'Were you expecting me to relieve you?'

'I thought *someone* might,' Nosjean said bitterly.

As Pel crept past to his office, he saw that the English tourist was back complaining that he hadn't yet had his wallet returned.

'It contained my French money, my English money, my traveller's cheques, my passport, my driving licence—'

Krauss was looking hopefully around for someone who could speak English better than he could.

'Yes, Monsieur,' he said. 'We have all that.'

'I must say, I don't think much of your city. I get talking to a perfectly respectable Frenchman and get myself robbed.'

'You went with him of your own accord, Monsieur.'

The Englishman avoided the point. 'Ever since I got here I've had people trying to put one across me. There was even this damn man in the car-park trying to get into my car.'

'Which man?'

'I don't know. Tall chap. Looked like an Italian.'

Pel stopped. 'You say he was trying to get into your car, Monsieur?' he asked in English.

The Englishman brightened. Obviously at last someone with some intelligence and authority was taking notice.

'Yes,' he said.

'He had the door open?'

'No. But he was prowling round, examining it—looking for a chance to get it open, I expect.'

Pel fished in the packet he was carrying and laid a photograph on the desk. 'Would that be the man, Monsieur?'

The Englishman looked up, startled by Pel's sudden interest. Then he gazed at the photograph. 'Yes,' he said. 'It would. But he looks different in this.'

'But, of course,' Pel said. 'He's dead.'

The Englishman's jaw dropped. 'Oh! What happened?'

'An accident. Did you speak to him?'

'Yes. I asked him what he was after.'

'And what did he say?'

'Just that he was interested in my car. He asked me if I was from Paris. When I said I wasn't he asked if the car parked next to me was from Paris.'

'Is that all he asked?'

'Yes.'

Pel looked at Darcy then back at the salesman. 'What exactly was he examining on your car? The engine? The tyres? The contents? The bodywork?'

'No.' The Englishman looked puzzled. 'The number plate.'

* * *

Reaching his office, Pel sat down in a thoughtful mood. Finishing the reports and the duty lists, he saw Sergeant Krauss and Sergeant Misset and fended off the indignant Nosjean who was determined to put in a complaint, then he reached for the telephone. The operator answered and Pel pulled forward his notebook.

'Keep this line clear,' he said. 'I have several long-distance calls to make.'

When Darcy arrived, Pel had finished his telephoning and was sitting quietly behind his desk, browsing through Nosjean's report on Barbièry.

'The lad said you wanted to see me, Chief.'

'That's right. I want you along with me. We're going to the Chenandier house.'

'To see Quermel?'

Pel didn't answer and Darcy didn't press him. They had both been up into the early hours of the morning and were both tired. They walked silently through the outer office and down the steps to the car-park. Neither of them spoke on the drive out to Aigunay and, stopping the car in the Chemin de Champ-Loups, they climbed out in silence and walked up the drive. They could see Odile Chenandier in the kitchen talking to Madame Quermel but, to Darcy's surprise, instead of heading for the door, Pel walked past the house and headed for the garden. Watched by the two women through the kitchen window, they moved across the lawn to the ivy-covered sheds by the stream. Followed by the puzzled Darcy, Pel pushed inside the one where the gardener had made a habit of eating his meal and began to peer at Albertini's wall scribblings. They had been added to over a long time and many of them had been written at an angle over earlier ones. There were a lot of crossings out and several were smudged by muddy finger marks.

'What are we looking for, Patron?' Darcy said.

'A number.'

'Telephone number?'

'No.'

Pel was in his secretive mood so Darcy didn't press the point. Eventually Pel wrote something in his notebook, peered at the wall again, checked what he saw among the mass of scribblings with what he'd written, then backed out of the shed.

'What now, Patron?' Darcy said 'Quermel?'

'No,' Pel said. 'I have other things to do.'

'Shall I see her for you?'

Pel shook his head. 'Leave her for the time being,' he said. 'We'll talk to her tonight. Late. In the meantime, have that lot photographed.'

'Which lot, Chief?'

Pel gestured at the scribblings. 'That lot,' he said. 'All of it. And make sure they make a good job of it. It's evidence.'

Darcy stared at the wall. 'What of, Chief?'

'A tidy mind,' Pel said.

Still puzzled, Darcy drove Pel back to the city. At headquarters, Pel disappeared into his own office and closed the door. Recognising his wish to be alone, Darcy headed for the sergeants' room. Nosjean's dulcet obbligato was still filling the air with his woes.

'I was here half the night,' he was complaining. 'I feel dead.'

'You look it,' Darcy said unsympathetically.

'My girl's threatened to chuck me. We were just in a clinch when you phoned.'

'Horrible.' Darcy shuddered. 'Shatters your nerves, that sort of thing. Like stopping taking opium.'

Nosjean scowled. 'You're pulling my leg,' he said.

'I know.' Darcy grinned. 'I hope some swine knocks me over the head with a blackjack so you'll be able to tell everybody what a rat I am.' He glanced towards Pel's office. 'Wonder what the old bastard's up to now.'

The 'old bastard' was on the telephone to Inspector Pomereu of Traffic. His eyes were glittering and he kept nodding as if at the back of his mind the tumblers of a combination lock were falling into place.

'That hit and run last night,' he was saying. 'I think I know where you can find the car.'

Pomereu sounded startled. 'Somebody you know?' he asked.

'I think so.'

'Then we'd better go and see the owner, hadn't we? Quick.'

'No,' Pel said. 'Don't go near the owner. Just check the car, that's all, and report back to me.'

'What are we looking for?'

'Red paint. There ought to be some on it from the motorbike the Italian rode. Just quietly sniff round it and ring me back. I think you'll find it in the car-park at this address—'

Pomereu's reply hadn't come when Pel left the office and he had to leave a message for it to be put through to his home. But nothing had arrived by dinner-time so, taking a glass of wine into the garden, he tried to relax and even fell into a doze. Unfortunately Madame Routy elected to do the ironing on the terrasse, assisted by Didier, two neighbours and their children, and as it dawned on her where Pel was, she shrieked a warning in a piercing whisper. 'Be quiet,' she yelled. 'He's asleep!' It was enough to wake the dead.

By the late evening, Pel was fretful and fidgety and when eventually Inspector Pomereu was put through he snatched at the telephone as though he were expecting the news of an invasion from outer space.

'Where the devil have you been?'

The voice at the other end was calm and unperturbed. 'Looking for the car.'

'I gave you the exact place!'

A faint hint of superiority came down the line. 'Indeed you did. But it wasn't there.'

'It wasn't?' Pel felt his heart thud into the pit of his stomach. 'Where's it got to then?'

'Don't get alarmed.' Pomereu's self-satisfaction literally oozed from the telephone. 'We found it. The chap who keeps an eye on the cars told us. It was in a little garage on the Lyon road. It's been used before and the car-park attendant once delivered it there for the owner. A couple of brothers called Orbeaux run it. It's part of the Laye outfit. They're not particular how they get their money, and they admitted accepting 5,000 frs to do the job and say nothing.'

'What was the job?'

'What you expected. Broken headlight glass, scratch marks on the right wing and fender. There was a lot of red paint.'

CHAPTER
SEVENTEEN

Half an hour later Pel had dug out Sergeant Darcy and they were heading out of the city. Darcy looked tired but he seemed to be enjoying a private joke.

'Well, go on,' Pel said. 'What's it all about?'

Darcy chuckled. 'You'll never guess. Nosjean's girl-friend's thrown him over.'

'And that's funny?'

'No. Not that. I think he's got another.'

'That's quick. Is she pretty?'

'Not specially. But I saw them talking in the car-park this afternoon and I must admit she looked different.'

'Who is it? One of the typists?'

'No. Odile Chenandier.'

Pel said nothing. In a strange way he felt better. Life had a habit of producing something worthwhile occasionally. Nosjean was an ardent young man and he just hoped that Odile would get some pleasure out of his company.

'We'll call at the station at Aigunay as we pass,' he said. 'To pick up a couple of men.'

'Why, Chief?'

'We might need them. I warned them to stand by.'

Darcy was silent for a while then he looked at Pel. 'I think you know who did it, Patron,' he said.

'Yes,' Pel agreed. 'I do.'

'Who?'

'It's not a question of who,' Pel said. 'It's more a question of "how". I've been puzzled by that all along. I couldn't make out how the house was entered, the woman murdered and the house left again without the murderer being covered with blood. It's pretty simple really, though, when you know.'

Darcy glanced sideways. 'Well, how?' he said.

Pel shrugged. 'Well,' he said, 'it was either a burglar or a tramp who was disturbed, or someone who bore her a grudge, wasn't it? And if it was someone who bore her a grudge, it was someone she knew.'

'But all that blood, Patron? Nobody involved in that mess could have entered the house and left in the ordinary way.'

'This one did.'

'But what about clothes?'

'There weren't any.'

Darcy stared long enough at Pel for the car to wander from the right of the road to the left. He wrenched it back. 'There weren't any?'

'The only way to avoid getting blood all over your clothes is to take 'em off.'

'There were—' Darcy glanced again at Pel. 'The doc said there was no sign of recent sexual intercourse.'

'No. No intercourse.'

'Well, you don't take your clothes off to pick a fight with someone. If you did, they'd probably die laughing.'

'She probably did die laughing,' Pel said dryly. 'But there was no passion in it. Either way. It wasn't a quarrel. It was premeditated. And it wasn't an intruder going for jewels. In fact, the jewels weren't even stolen, were they?—except by Odile.'

'But naked, Patron! Without a stitch on! It'd have to be without a stitch.'

'It was.'

'Who?'

'If you can walk into a house without clothes on, as this one did, you'd have to be well-known to the murdered woman, wouldn't you?'

'Go on, Patron.'

Pel lit a cigarette and passed the packet across. 'It might have been Odile,' he said. 'I thought of her and wondered if she'd done it for the jewels. She certainly knew exactly what there was and where they were. And it wouldn't seem wildly crazy to her mother to see her without clothes—or perhaps in the briefest of underclothes—would it? Odd, but not mad.'

'Patron, I checked her flat for bloodstains and blood-stained clothes. There was nothing.'

Pel nodded and Darcy went on. 'And it wouldn't be Estelle Quermel,' he said. 'Housekeepers don't usually walk around in their skin in front of their employers.'

'Not unless there was some odd sexual interest.' Pel peered through the windscreen at the road winding ahead of them in the lights. 'And these days you have to consider these things. There are some funny people about.' He sniffed disapprovingly and went on. 'And if there *were* some special interest of that sort, then it *wouldn't* disturb Madame Chenandier, would it? But that wasn't the way it was done either. Who'd be least likely to startle a woman by wearing no clothes? Two people: her husband—or her lover.'

'Laye!' Darcy grinned. 'She was having an affair with him so she must have seen *him* without his clothes.'

'According to Laye's daughter, she had,' Pel said. 'He had me puzzled for a long time because he was the same shape and size as Chenandier, had the same kind of car, and could easily be mistaken for him. In fact, the gardener *did* mistake him—in the lane. I felt it must have been one of them but I never really knew which until this morning. Laye even had an office in Bazay where Albertini lived and that suggested a connection straight away.'

'How was it done, Patron?'

'The murderer entered the house naked. There was a struggle and he ran out.' Pel made it sound as simple as crossing the road, and Darcy frowned.

'But, Patron, there must have been blood all over his body. When he put his clothes on again, they'd have been marked.'

'Agreed,' Pel said. 'But he didn't put his clothes on. Not until he'd taken a bath.'

'Where? You can't run down the lane stark naked. Not even to next door. Or up the stairs. So where did he take a bath? There'd have been traces of blood somewhere.'

'There were,' Pel pointed out. 'In the garden, you remember. But not many, because the rain washed them away. It poured that night. It was the hit and run that told me what had happened.'

Darcy drew a deep breath. 'Near Laye's office at Bazay,' he said. 'Was it Laye?'

'It's not a bad guess,' Pel said cheerfully. 'Because it connects up with the office in Bazay and being in the Chemin de Champ-Loups at the right time. And certainly whoever hit Albertini with a car killed Madame Chenandier. Now that Albertini's dead there'll be two charges of murder. One with a blunt instrument. One with a wheeled vehicle.'

Darcy was still baffled. 'But how was it done? All that blood. Where did it go?'

'I couldn't work that out,' Pel admitted. 'Not until yesterday when I saw a small boy strip to go into the river to fish out a hook caught in the reeds. He did it to avoid getting mud on his clothes. Then I knew at once. He'd worked it all out ahead. He arrived outside the house wearing only something to cover him, gloves and shoes, and entered by the front door, leaving them outside. When Madame Chenandier saw him she probably burst out laughing because he was wearing nothing but a pair of gloves.' Pel shrugged. 'I don't suppose she laughed for long.'

Darcy was still puzzled. 'But the blood, Chief? How did he get rid of it?'

'He went out through the french windows. The bath was right there. A few yards away. Waiting for him.'

'The stream!' Darcy drew his breath sharply.

'Exactly. He knew he couldn't be seen from the houses on either side and could run down the garden stark naked. At the stream, he flung the poker away. So it would be found and look as if an intruder had done it. He knew quite

well he could take his time bathing because he couldn't be
seen, and at the other side of the stream his clothes were
waiting. It seemed from the beginning it was Laye, because
of the office at Bazay and the fact that he could walk along
the stream to his own garden if he wished, and climb out
there, washed, clean and ready to face anybody who came.
His house was even empty that night. His whole family was
out.'

Pel became silent and Darcy looked quickly at him. His
features were caught by the dashboard light and he was
wearing a smug look.

'But it wasn't Laye,' he said eventually. 'It was Chenandier.'

Darcy's head turned again. 'Chenandier?'

Pel shrugged. 'Well, a man doesn't murder his wife when
he's been indifferent to her for years. But if another woman
appears and wants him to marry *her*, it changes the picture a
bit, doesn't it?'

'But, Chief, he was in Paris! He must have been in Paris!
He couldn't use the train and his car was at the station every
bit of the time.'

'He didn't use the train. And his car *was* at the station all
the time.' Pel opened the window to toss away his cigarette
end. 'He used a hire car from Paris. Luxe Cars, of Rue
Henri-Padac. One of Laye's companies. He probably used
them because his wife and Laye were known to them and he
wasn't, and he thought it might throw suspicion the wrong
way. I checked with them this morning. He hired it by
telephone to go to Rennes and got a student from the
Alliance Française called Berthelo to pick it up and deliver
it to him at a prearranged rendezvous near the Closerie des
Lilas. I got that too. The boy volunteered the information
willingly enough when the question was asked around by
the Quai des Orfèvres. He was innocent enough. But the
car didn't go to Rennes. Luxe Cars thought it did because
the mileage was right.' He paused. 'The mileage would also
be right if he'd driven here.'

'And he did?'

'Down the motorway, I expect. It's only a four-hour drive if you hurry. Especially in the evening when it's quiet.'

Darcy was silent and Pel went on quietly. 'He'd armed himself ahead with a theatre ticket from the Bobino,' he said. 'Probably bought at the booking office the night before. He did what he had to do then drove back. Down in the evening, and back after dark. He undressed in the car and left it in the shadows at the bottom of the Chemin de Champ-Loups. He walked to the house wearing shoes, gloves and the plastic mac from his suitcase which, in the dark, would seem opaque and would cover him from shoulders to calves. The lane was deserted, as he knew it would be, because there are only three houses and few people went down there. Afterwards, he bathed in the stream and, because it was cold, put on a tracksuit that must have been waiting for him, while he cleaned up some more.'

'The one the gardener mentioned?'

'Exactly. I was thinking of waterproofs all the time because of the rain and was looking all over the place for an anorak to account for the zips Nosjean found. And because I'd got my mind set on an anorak and because Chenandier had never owned one I thought it was Laye who'd done it, because *he* did own one. Then when I saw that kid in the red tracksuit who did the supermarket at Talant I suddenly remembered the gardener saying he'd seen Chenandier in a tracksuit, having a necking session with Quermel. Then I realised that was where the zips Nosjean found in the fire came from. Because he was meticulous he'd also brought a thick sweater, but it wasn't as cold as he'd expected and because he was always a bit careful with his money and he hadn't worn the sweater and it wasn't touched by blood, he didn't need to throw it away.

'However, the stream comes down from the hills and it's chilly even on a warm day so he did drink the brandy that was waiting for him—some to give him courage, some after it was over to warm him. He then drove back to Paris; and Berthelo, the student from the Alliance Française who'd picked up the car for him, met him and took it back. The boys from the Quai des Orfèvres have impounded it and I expect they'll find his fingerprints on it somewhere. There was no blood. I asked Luxe Cars.'

Darcy was silent again and Pel went on quickly. 'He arrived back at his hotel the morning after the murder—early, and looking clean and smart as if he'd just got up. He appeared in the hall as if he'd been out to buy a paper and even complaining he couldn't get what he wanted, to draw attention to himself. He was quite unmarked by blood by now and looking as if he'd never been out of the capital. He'd probably even taken another bath at some woman's.'

'He'd got a nerve, Chief.'

'Yes. He went to Paris prepared for it all because the desk clerk at the Meurice thought he had a black bag when he arrived but couldn't remember seeing one when he left. I checked the house later and found no black bag—or track-suit—so he probably used the bag to carry the track suit to Paris when he first went and dumped it later in the Seine. Probably the frogmen will find it.'

Darcy shifted behind the wheel, his eyes on the road. 'And then?'

'And then he went on with his affairs in Paris and spent a normal day until the evening. In the evening he pretended to learn of the murder from the papers, asked for his bill and caught the early train down the next day, picking up his car in the ordinary way.'

Darcy frowned. 'He was working to a pretty tight schedule, Patron,' he said. 'He had to burn the tracksuit and the gloves before he set off back north. And what about the plastic mac and the shoes he left on the doorstep?'

'Not too difficult. He had some help.'

'Quermel?'

'She probably also helped him drink the brandy—to steady her nerves.'

'What makes you think she's involved?'

Pel was silent for a while. 'Your telephone call last evening,' he said. 'It was Chenandier who ran down the gardener.'

'You sure, Chief?'

'I am now. The car he hired in Paris was in the lane the
night of the murder. It was tucked away in the shadows
where it becomes a footpath. Three people said so—Darcq,
Laye and Laye's daughter. They thought it was dark blue or
black. In fact, it was dark green, but it would look black in
the shadows. They didn't go near it, though, because no
one goes down that lane much.' He paused. 'Except for one
person, who used that lane as a habit.'

'The gardener. To go home.'

Pel nodded. 'He went that way as usual that night, to his
sister's at Boux, and he was the only one who *could* go that
way, because he rode a motorbike and could drive it that
way on to the Langres road. He saw the car, though he
insisted he didn't. He even had a good look round it and
saw the strange number plate. It was written on the wall in
the shed where he ate. 1167-BR-75. The number of the
Peugeot that was hired in Paris.' Pel gestured. 'It puzzled
him. He'd noticed that all the numbers round here end in
21—Côte d'Or; 71—Saône et Loire; or 25—Doubs; with an
occasional 39 for the Jura or a 45 for Loiret. The number 75
made him think. Being Italian, he didn't know French
numbers well, so he asked around. He even tried Estelle
Quermel. Odile heard him.'

'And Quermel guessed what he was up to?'

'Not at the time,' Pel said. 'Our friend Albertini was
pretty crafty and, though he'd guessed she and Chenandier
were having an affair, he didn't suspect *she* was involved in
the murder. But he'd guessed what had happened. He
wasn't very bright but he was bright enough for that, and he
took care to write the number down.'

'Why?'

'Blackmail. He'd tried it once before, remember, and I
think he was going to try it again. Unfortunately, he never
got the chance. Chenandier found out and realised he was
in trouble. He followed him home when he left last evening.'

'How did he find out?'

'From the person who removed the plastic mackintosh

and shoes from the doorstep. The person who met him at the other side of the stream with the brandy—at a time when she claimed she was in the Cours de Gaulle—who poured paraffin on the gloves and the tracksuit when he took them off and set light to them, the only person Albertini asked about the numbers who *could* have passed it on to Chenandier.'

'Quermel?'

Pel nodded. 'She probably didn't associate Albertini's questions about car numbers with Chenandier until I asked her if she'd seen a strange car down the lane that night. Then she realised exactly what Albertini had been getting at, and told Chenandier. That signed Albertini's death warrant.'

CHAPTER EIGHTEEN

They had reached Aigunay now and the sergeant was waiting for them as the car pulled up at the police station.

'Message for you, sir,' he said. 'From one of your people. You're to ring Sergeant Nosjean.'

Pel glanced at Darcy and headed for the telephone. Nosjean sounded excited. 'I've just had Odile on the telephone, Chief—Odile Chenandier.'

'I heard you'd got a new girlfriend,' Pel said dryly.

'Not exactly a—' Nosjean started to explain then changed his mind. 'Listen, Chief, she sounded scared! It seems she saw her father's car come back last night. It had red paint on it and she'd heard about the gardener. She decided he'd done it.'

'He had.'

'Well, she's been putting one or two things together and she's worried sick. She wanted to see me. To talk to me.'

'What about?'

'I think she thinks it was her father who killed her mother and she's scared stiff he knows and might try to do something to *her*. She didn't say so, not outright, you understand, but I could read between the lines, as you might say.'

'You're cleverer than you look, Nosjean.'

'Chief—' Nosjean sounded worried '—can I come out there? It'll only take me half an hour.'

'Got transport?' Pel asked.

'My own car, Chief.'

'Then get moving.'

Pel was almost running when he came out once more to the car.

'On your way,' he snapped at Darcy. 'And make it fast!'

'Right, Chief!'

'Got your gun?'

'Yes.' Darcy glanced sideways. 'What's up, Chief?'

'Odile rang Nosjean. She thinks he's after *her* now.'

'He'd never try to do his own daughter in!'

Pel gestured irritably. Murder was an accumulative thing. One case invariably led to another, as this one had. A frightened man might do anything and a man who could plot so careful a murder as Chenandier had was possibly not wholly sane.

'He did his wife in,' he growled. 'Can't you go a bit faster?'

As they sped through the tunnel under the trees created by their own headlights, Pel was worried. Against his normal procedure, he had taken a curious liking to Odile. It was a liking composed chiefly of sympathy for her gracelessness and the feeling that, given the chance, she could find some happiness.

When the car drew to a stop in the Chemin de Champ-Loups, there were lights on in the Chenandier house. They rang the bell but there was no response.

Then quite clearly they heard Odile's voice, high-pitched and terrified. 'Go away! Oh, please go away!'

Pel gestured at the door. 'Break it in,' he said.

The first thing they saw as the door swung open was Madame Quermel. She was wearing a short housecoat and clearly wore nothing underneath.

'I was just going to have a bath,' she said nervously, but they knew at once she was lying. She looked scared and was clutching the newel post at the bottom of the stairs.

'Monsieur Chenandier?' Pel said.

Her mouth worked soundlessly and Pel gestured at the policeman. 'Upstairs,' he said. 'See if he's up there!' To the sergeant, he indicated the housekeeper. 'You stay here, sergeant. Keep an eye on her. Come with me, Darcy.'

Pushing through the house towards Odile Chenandier's flat, they almost bumped into Chenandier standing near the door. He was wearing pyjamas and a dressing gown and was leaning against the wall, one hand in his pocket. They stopped dead as they saw him, because it didn't take much effort to guess what he was holding. Chenandier eyed them with flickering eyes like a cornered animal.

'We'd like a few words with you, Monsieur,' Pel said.

Chenandier frowned. 'At this hour?'

'I'm afraid so.'

'What is it this time?'

'We'd like you to come into the city with us.'

'What for?'

'We have a few questions to ask you. You may have to make a statement.'

'What about?'

'I think you know.'

There was a slight sound like a gasp behind them and Pel looked round. Madame Quermel had appeared, followed by the sergeant.

'You, too, Madame,' Darcy said.

Chenandier stared at them, his eyes narrowing, his hand still in the pocket of his dressing gown.

Pel gestured at the door of the flat. 'What are you doing here?' he asked.

'I—' Chenandier's jaw worked '—my daughter—'

Pel stepped warily past him and tried the door. It was locked and, as he moved the handle, he heard Odile's voice scream.

'No! No! Go away!'

Pel paused. 'This is Inspector Pel,' he called. 'I think you can come out in just one moment.'

He turned to Chenandier. 'If you'll just hand over what you have in your pocket.'

Chenandier frowned, glancing about him, then suddenly he made a dive for the stairs. Madame Quermel went flying as he barged past. Falling to the floor, she slid on its polished surface to crash into a plant-stand and bring it down with a scattering of earth. As the sergeant stepped forward Chenandier wrenched at his pocket. They saw a glimpse of blue metal and, as the sergeant grappled with him, Chenandier swung at him with the gun and he fell back with a yell. Darcy was pulling at his own gun now but, as Chenandier leapt for the stairs, the policeman came crashing down from the floor above and the two of them collided on the turn and hurtled to the bottom together. Chenandier was on his feet first, the gun in his fist, but as he turned Darcy shot him in the shoulder.

He fell back against the stairs, bleeding; and, indifferent to Pel, the cursing sergeant, who was holding his mouth and spitting out broken teeth, and the policeman still lumbering to his feet, Madame Quermel fell on her knees beside him, holding his head to her breast and moaning with anguish.

Pel tapped on the door of the flat. 'It's safe now, Mademoiselle,' he said.

Drawing a deep breath, he lit a cigarette, feeling for once he deserved it and needed it and that this time God wouldn't strike him down with a thunderbolt for his bad habits. As he dragged the smoke down to his socks, they heard sobbing from the other side of the door. Darcy was about to force it open when Pel stopped him.

'Leave her,' he said. 'Let her get over it. When Nosjean arrives, you'd better send *him* in. He'll probably do more good than you or I.'

OUR RECORD OF PREVIOUS CRIMES

Some of the exciting tales of murder, mystery,
danger, detection and suspense already
published in Keyhole Crime.

EXPENDABLE   *Willo Davis Roberts*
NOWHERE?   *Aaron Marc Stein*
DEATH IN THE ROUND   *Anne Morice*
THE CHIEF INSPECTOR'S DAUGHTER
   Sheila Radley
DEATH BY BEQUEST   *Mary McMullen*
A POCKET FULL OF DEAD   *John Wyllie*
THE INCOMER   *Graham Gaunt*
BEYOND THIS POINT ARE MONSTERS
   Margaret Millar
POSTHUMOUS PAPERS   *Robert Barnard*
THE LIME PIT   *Jonathan Valin*
DOUBLE BLUFF   *Dell Shannon*
IN COLD PURSUIT   *Ursula Curtiss*
AN AMATEUR CORPSE   *Simon Brett*
THE IMPOSTER   *Helen McCloy*
THE RIDGWAY WOMEN   *Richard Neely*
RALLY TO KILL   *Bill Knox*

Look out for them wherever you normally buy paperbacks

 Keyhole Crime

If you have any difficulty obtaining any of these
titles, or if you would like further information on
forthcoming titles in Keyhole Crime please write to:-
Keyhole Crime, PO Box 236, Thornton Road,
Croydon, Surrey CR9 3RU.

NOW READ ON WITH KEYHOLE CRIME
Other titles available in the shops now

THE DEADEST THING YOU EVER SAW
Jonathan Ross

Michael Clancy was found hanging from a tree with a
paper bag over his head and his wrist and ankles tied
together with string. Clearly, it was a ritual killing.

Clancy had just served an absurdly short sentence for rape
and murder and it looked to Detective Inspector Rogers as
if his two accomplices might well be next on some
revenger's list. But it took an odd interview and a second
execution before Roger's came to the hair-raising finale.

EVERY SECOND THURSDAY
Emma Page

Vera Foster led a very enclosed life. She had no close
women friends, no relatives, scarcely any visitors — and
when she was found dead from an overdose, the verdict
was suicide. After all, she'd tried it once before.

But one small sign after the inquest aroused Detective
Chief Inspector Kelsey's suspicions. Although the case
was officially closed, he continued investigations . . . even
though two lives could be permanently ruined and he
himself might face professional disaster . . .

 **Keyhole Crime**

NOW READ ON WITH KEYHOLE CRIME

Other titles available in the shops now

ONE DIP DEAD
Aaron Marc Stein

Matt Erridge and trouble seemed to go together like ham and eggs, fish and chips or love and marriage — only this time the scene was Easter Sunday in Florence where Erridge was attending mass in the Duomo with an attractive widow and her daughter.

Nobody in the huge crowd heard the shot when it came or actually saw the dead man as he fell — where else but opposite Erridge? And where else should the murder weapon be found but planted in Matt's pocket? He ate his easter dinner in jail . . .

THE MAN WITH FIFTY COMPLAINTS
Mary McMullen

For twenty-five years, Lester had been a loyal, if somewhat inconspicuous employee of Bela Industries, until the day he saw quite clearly that he had no place to go in the foreseeable future. Suddenly his whole life became focused on revenge and he began a catalogue of the 'deplorable practices' of Bela employees — expecting at least a nod of thanks from Head Office, but not expecting to attract the dangerous fury of his colleagues . . .

Look out for them wherever you normally buy paperbacks

 Keyhole Crime